He leaned back and stretched his legs in front of him. The denim of his jeans rubbed against her bare legs. Her breath caught.

Usually that was a warning sign of an all-too-frequent panic attack. But it wasn't anxiety that caused the tingly sensation deep inside her tonight.

She was so not ready for this with Luke or any other man. "I should probably go see if I can help in the kitchen," she said.

"Why do I get the feeling you're trying to get rid of me?"

"You're welcome in the kitchen."

"Thanks, but I guess I'll go out back with the guys and trade in my empty beer bottle for a full one."

"Good idea."

They both stood.

He tipped his hat. "Nice chatting with you, Rachel Maxwell. I still think there's a mystery that I need to get to the bottom of."

And that was it. He walked away while she was fighting the effect he was having on her.

DROPPING
THE HAMMER

JOANNA WAYNE

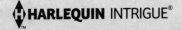
HARLEQUIN INTRIGUE®

To the people in southeast Texas who not only survived Hurricane Harvey but showed amazing gusto in pitching in to help friends and absolute strangers who suffered devastating losses. And to the people around the state, country and the world who supported the relief efforts with their time, money and prayers. Your spirit of love and caring will never be forgotten.

ISBN-13: 978-1-335-52630-4

Dropping the Hammer

Copyright © 2018 by Jo Ann Vest

Recycling programs for this product may not exist in your area.

Printed in U.S.A.

Joanna Wayne began her professional writing career in 1994. Now, more than fifty published books later, Joanna has gained a worldwide following with her cutting-edge romantic suspense and Texas family series, such as Sons of Troy Ledger and Big "D" Dads. Joanna currently resides in a small community north of Houston, Texas, with her husband. You may write Joanna at PO Box 852, Montgomery, TX 77356, or connect with her at joannawayne.com.

Books by Joanna Wayne

Harlequin Intrigue

The Kavanaughs

Riding Shotgun
Quick-Draw Cowboy
Fearless Gunfighter
Dropping the Hammer

Big "D" Dads: The Daltons

Trumped Up Charges
Unrepentant Cowboy
Hard Ride to Dry Gulch
Midnight Rider
Showdown at Shadow Junction
Ambush at Dry Gulch

Sons of Troy Ledger

Cowboy Swagger
Genuine Cowboy
AK-Cowboy
Cowboy Fever
Cowboy Conspiracy

Big "D" Dads

Son of a Gun
Live Ammo
Big Shot

Visit the Author Profile page at Harlequin.com.

CAST OF CHARACTERS

Rachel Maxwell—Recovering from an abduction and torturous captivity, she is determined to fight her way back from the haunting fear and memories.

Luke Dawkins—He returns to the family ranch in Winding Creek to deal with an ailing father, only to become involved with the troubled and beautiful Rachel Maxwell.

Alfred Dawkins—Luke's father.

Eric Fitch, Sr.—Rachel's controlling boss at the Fitch, Fitch and Bauman law firm.

Roy Sales—The man who abducted Rachel and others.

Dr. Kincaid—Roy Sales's psychiatrist.

Hayden Covey—Accused of brutally murdering his former girlfriend, he is determined to have Rachel defend him.

Senator and Claire Covey—Hayden's wealthy and politically influential parents.

Sydney Lawrence—Rachel's FBI agent sister, who only wants to protect Rachel from looming danger.

Tucker Lawrence—Sydney's husband, a championship bull rider and one of the three Lawrence brothers who have come back to live in Winding Creek. Tucker, Riley and Pierce lived with Esther and Charlie Kavanaugh for a brief period after their parents were killed in a car wreck while the brothers were in high school.

Esther Kavanaugh—She's always there to lend a helping hand and is the best cook in the county.

Prologue

Death screamed, echoing shrilly through Rachel Maxwell's brain as Roy Sales's large, meaty hands tightened around her throat. His powerful body was stretched on top of hers, pinning her to her bed.

Her chest burned. She couldn't breathe. She was losing consciousness as fear clawed at her insides, tearing her apart bit by bloody bit. Even as life slipped away, her heart persisted, throbbing erratically.

"Don't worry, sweet Rachel. I won't let you die if you do what I say."

His maniacal laugh crawled inside her as his grip on her throat slowly eased. She coughed, choking as oxygen fought its way back into her lungs.

"Bucking against me is futile, sweetheart. I'll never let you go. You belong to me. You always will. You know you want it that way."

"Let me go," she pleaded, her voice dry and scratchy, little more than a whisper. "Please, let me go."

"That's the way, baby. Keep begging."

She closed her eyes tight so that she didn't have to see the evil that darkened his eyes. Pleading wouldn't help. He was heartless, devoid of compassion, his deranged soul as black as the depths of the deepest cave.

She writhed and twisted beneath him, finally getting her right arm free. She fisted her hand and swung wildly.

Blunt pain met her knuckles. There was a crash. She cried out in pain as blood splattered her face and dripped through her fingers.

She managed a scream. Loud. Shrill.

Her body stiffened and she kicked wildly, her feet tangling in the sheets as she escaped his grasping hands. Still screaming, she jerked into wakefulness— not to the sound of her cries, but to her cell phone's alarm.

Rachel gulped scratchy clumps of air. It was only a nightmare. She was in her own apartment. Alone. Safe.

She fumbled to turn off the alarm. Her phone was wet. Her hands were damp and clammy, but with water, not the blood she'd imagined in the clutches of the terrifying nightmare.

She'd evidently knocked over the glass of water she'd left on the bedside table. The dizziness and cold, hard terror began to subside as she dried her phone on the corner of the sheet.

She stretched her feet out in front of her, staring at the shadows that crawled across the wall in the faint glow of sunrise. She was safe and yet the horror of being kidnapped and held in captivity by the psychopath persisted along with anxiety attacks and sudden bouts of panic.

Something as routine as a strange man walking too close behind her in downtown Houston in broad daylight could set her off. Or a man approaching in the office parking lot. Or even the creepy feeling that someone was watching her when she got out of her car at night.

She had to get her act together and move past her own trauma. But even fully awake and in the safety of her own bedroom, she could feel killing fingers at her throat, choking the life from her.

She could sense danger deep in her soul.

Chapter One

Three months later

"Good morning, Miss Maxwell."

The firm's receptionist smiled as Rachel walked through the double glass doors of their fifteenth-floor office.

"You're here early this morning, Carrie," Rachel said.

"Yes, but it may be the first time I've ever arrived before you. Sometimes I think you sleep here."

"I've been tempted."

"Mr. Fitch Sr. beat you in this morning, too. He said to have you stop by his office when you arrived."

"Did he say why?"

"No, but I got the idea it's important."

Everything was important to Eric Fitch Sr. He had a controlling hand over everything that went on in this firm.

Rachel stopped by her office, shrugged out of her

light gray overcoat and put it and her handbag away before heading to Eric's office.

His door was ajar. She tapped on it and he stood and motioned her inside.

"Carrie said you needed to see me?"

"Yes. It's going to be a very busy and hopefully productive day. If you have any appointments that aren't urgent, you'll need to cancel them."

"Sounds serious. What's up?"

"We have a potential very high-profile case I'd like to discuss with you."

Rachel couldn't imagine why he wanted to discuss that with her. She took the chair that faced his desk. He sat down again and leaned back in his oversize leather chair.

"Who's the defendant?" she asked.

"Hayden Covey. I suppose you've heard that he was arrested last night."

"It was breaking news on my phone alerts this morning." She was certain almost everyone in the state had heard by now.

Hayden was a student at University of Texas who'd allegedly brutally murdered his girlfriend days after she'd broken up with him.

He was also the only son of a popular and very influential state senator married to an extremely rich heiress.

The victim was Louann Black, nineteen years old,

also a student at the university. Though not as wealthy and influential as the Coveys, her family was well-known in the Austin music circuit.

Hayden had written several songs for big-name performers and frequently performed around town himself in popular music venues.

This would likely be the trial of the decade in Texas.

"Do you think Hayden is innocent?" Rachel asked.

"He claims to be and I know his parents believe him."

"Most parents do, though the evidence against him looks extremely damaging."

"But not ironclad," Eric said. "A top-notch defense attorney could win the case."

"Then coming to you was a good decision," Rachel said. "Few would argue that you're not the top defense attorney in the South."

"But maybe not the best man to defend Hayden. I'll be honest with you, Rachel. Senator Covey and I have been close friends since our law school days at UT. I've known Hayden since he was born. He's a great kid."

"He's twenty," Rachel reminded him. "Not exactly a kid."

"That's true. He's turned into a fine young man with a great life and a pro football career in front of him. He's one of the top college running backs in the country and he's only a junior."

"Even great athletes commit crimes."

"Yes, but he's never been in trouble except for one unfortunate arrest last year for roughing up another student after an altercation at a bar near the university. Several witnesses said the victim was at fault."

According to the media over the last few days, those witnesses were Hayden's friends and the *roughing up* was a vicious attack that sent an unsuspecting underclassman to the hospital with a broken jaw and a serious concussion from repeated kicks to the head.

That was nothing compared to the brutality of the attack that killed his former girlfriend.

"Considering how my friendship with the senator might negatively influence the jury, I'm not sure I'm the best one to officially lead Hayden's defense."

"Good point," she agreed, though she was certain he'd be a strong behind-the-scenes force in the case no matter who was the lead attorney of record.

"Luckily, the firm has several top-notch criminal defense attorneys," she noted.

"Yes, which makes this a tough decision. But I talked with my son and Edward last evening. We all three believe that you're the best choice for the job."

She stared at him, stunned by his words. "You mean as lead attorney?"

"Yes, though you'll have full backing from the

firm and all the assistance you require. But you'll deliver the opening and closing statements and handle the press."

She'd worked her butt off for an opportunity like this ever since she started with the firm right after law school. But she was certain her performance had fallen off over the last few months. She tried harder than ever, but she had trouble concentrating and dealing with the never-ending panic attacks.

"Why me?" she asked.

"I've discussed it with my partners. We all agree that you have exactly the qualities needed for this trial. You're not only capable and thorough, you read the jury as well as or better than any attorney with the firm. You proved that time and time again."

"I've never headed up a high-profile like this."

"No, but you've demonstrated that you know your way around a courtroom. You won't be intimidated by a judge or daunted by the best the district attorney can hurl at you."

A year ago that might have been the case. Now she wasn't convinced she could navigate through all the brutal murder evidence and still stay on her game.

She'd only been a team member on the case they'd just tried and won, but even looking at the photos of a young female victim attacked in an elevator at her workplace had brought on an increase in Rachel's nightmares and a heightened anxiety level.

Her career had been her life, but it seemed to be turning on her. She definitely couldn't handle a murder case unless she was totally convinced of the defendant's innocence. "I appreciate the confidence, but—"

"I know it will be your biggest challenge to date," Fitch interrupted. "We think you're ready for it."

She stared into space as she let his statement sink in. What-ifs stormed her mind. What if she wasn't up to it? What if she wasn't convinced of Hayden Covey's innocence? What if she had a meltdown in front of the jury? If that happened in a case this high profile, it would be the end of her career.

Eric stood, walked to the front of his desk and stared down at her, his gaze intent, intimidating. "This case is very important to me and to the firm, Rachel. We've stood beside you and supported you in every way we could since your unfortunate incident. Now I'm asking for you to deliver. Don't let me down."

Don't let him down.

The tone and stance made it clear his words were a warning. This was more than an offer. It was a demand.

"I understand," she said.

"Good. Then I've made myself clear."

"Perfectly clear. When do I meet the defendant?" she asked, though she hadn't officially agreed to take the assignment. Ordinarily, the firm granted attorneys that privilege. This time that didn't appear to be the case.

"Hayden and his parents will be here this morning at ten," Fitch said. "I'll also sit in on that first meeting."

"I expected that you would. Is that all for now?"

"Yes, except that I should warn you that Hayden's mother, Claire, is in a distraught state. I hope you can give her full confidence in the defense we'll provide for her son."

"I'll do as much as I honestly can." Honestly was the key word in Rachel's mind.

Eric Fitch Sr. had gotten what he wanted. He stood, then smiled and nodded, acknowledging his win.

Rachel was getting the career boost she'd worked so hard for, the opportunity to make a name for herself and vastly improve her chance of being named at least a junior partner one day soon.

So why did she feel the almost overwhelming desire to tell Eric Fitch he could take this job and shove it?

Chapter Two

Luke Dawkins nudged his worn Stetson back on his head and took a long, hard look at the rusting metal gate. Arrowhead Hills Ranch was carved into the weathered wooden sign along with two imprints of arrowheads.

The last time he'd laid eyes on that gate, he'd seen it through the rearview mirror of the beat-up red pickup truck that he'd bought with money he'd earned working at the local feed and tack shop. That had been eleven years ago, when he was eighteen.

The rickety ranch gate seemed the same. Luke wasn't.

You Can't Go Home Again. Thomas Wolfe had known his stuff. The home might not change. The person who'd left would.

A few years of bouncing from job to job followed by eight years in the military had turned Luke into a man, yet he still dreaded returning to the place he'd once called home.

A small Texas Hill Country town with a lot more cows than people, more barbwire than roads and some of the best ranch land in the state.

All Luke had against the town or the ranch could be summed up in two words. Alfred Dawkins. Stubborn. Controlling. Bitter. Downright ornery.

The poor excuse for a father wouldn't like having Luke home again any more than Luke wanted to be here.

Neither of them had a lot of choice in the matter.

The old defiant angers festered in Luke's gut as he climbed out of his new double-cab pickup truck and stepped around a mud hole.

His boots scooted across the cattle gap as he unlatched and opened the gate before getting back into his truck and driving through it the way he'd done hundreds of times as a rebellious teenager.

He paused and took in the sights and sounds before he closed the gate behind him. A barking dog, though it wouldn't be Ace, the golden retriever he'd raised from a pup. Ace had died from a rattlesnake bite when he jumped between Luke and the striking snake.

Luke had been fourteen then. His dad had scorned him for shedding a few tears. Nothing new. Luke had never measured up in his dad's mind. Just one of the many reasons Luke had never looked back once he left Arrowhead Hills Ranch.

A crow scolded Luke from high in the branches of a nearby live oak. A horse neighed.

Luke looked to the left and spotted a couple of chestnut mares giving him the once-over. So his dad still kept horses. Good to know.

It had been years since Luke was in the saddle. His consecutive tours in the Middle East hadn't allowed much time for revisiting the cowboy lifestyle.

It was shirtsleeve weather, warm for late January, but a bracing breeze rustled the tall yellow strands of grass and the leaves in a persimmon tree that hugged the fence.

Luke closed the gate, climbed back into his truck and drove toward the old house. He had no idea what to expect or what kind of health his father had been in before he suffered the stroke that had led to his being placed in a rehab facility.

Significantly weakened on the left side of his body now and with difficulty putting his thoughts into coherent sentences, he was unable to take care of himself, much less the ranch.

Not that Luke had originally gotten that information firsthand. It was Esther Kavanaugh, a longtime neighbor who'd been his mother's best friend before her death, who'd called with the SOS. Luke had followed up with Alfred's doctor and the rehab center.

So here he was, back in Winding Creek.

The brown roof appeared as he rounded a curve

in the dirt ranch road. Trees hid the rest of the clap-board house until he was closer.

It looked smaller than he remembered it. A bun-galow with two bedrooms, two baths, a family den, a large kitchen downstairs and an upstairs dormer with another bedroom and bath that had been his hideaway.

Luke parked in a gravel drive in front of the car-port that covered what he assumed was his dad's scratched and dented Chevy pickup truck. Alfred had always been a Chevy man and always hard on the finish of the vehicle. He'd never let bushes or shrubs get in the way of his getting where he wanted to go on the ranch.

The wide, covered porch that his mother had al-ways filled with huge clay pots of colorful blooms was bare except for one old pottery planter full of dirt and dead flowers, a weathered wooden rocker and what looked to be a fairly new porch swing that dangled from the ceiling by only one chain.

Luke's mother's once prized flower beds that had bordered the porch were choked with weeds. The paint on the house was faded and peeling. A dark brown shutter on one of the windows hung askew.

Luke climbed out of the truck and took the cracked concrete walk from the driveway to the porch steps. A sense of foreboding rattled his mood. Stepping back into the house with its bittersweet memories of his mother would have been depressing in an ideal situation. This was far from ideal.

He had no idea what Alfred or the neighbors expected of him. He didn't mind the work, but it wasn't as if he had any authority to make decisions about the ranch. More than likely his father hadn't even named him in the will even though Luke had no siblings.

The door was unlocked. Luke swung it open, but before he could step inside, he heard approaching hoofbeats. He turned as the horseman rode into view, pulled on the reins and stopped in the shade a few yards from the porch.

The black mare snorted and tossed her head as the rider climbed from the saddle and looped the reins around a low-lying branch of a scraggly ash tree.

The rider acknowledged Luke with a smile and a nod.

Luke tipped his Stetson.

"You must be Luke," the cowboy said as he approached the porch steps. "Esther Kavanaugh said you'd be here sometime this weekend. She wasn't sure when, so I was just coming by to see if you made it yet."

"Yep. Luke Dawkins. Just drove up. Haven't even made it inside." He met the guy on the edge of the porch and offered his hand.

"Buck Stalling," the guy said. "I'm a wrangler for Pierce Lawrence over at the Double K Ranch.

He sends me over here twice a day to take care of the horses."

"Is Pierce running the ranch for Esther Kavanaugh now?" Luke asked.

"He owns it. Mrs. Kavanaugh sold it to him a few months back."

"Interesting. She didn't mention that she'd moved when I talked to her."

"She didn't move. She lives right there in the big house like she always has, close to her beloved chickens and garden."

"Does Pierce live there, too?"

"He did before he built himself, his pregnant wife, Grace, and his young daughter a house of their own no more than a good stone's throw away from Esther. Right nice setup."

"Sounds like a good deal for all of them. I just didn't realize Pierce was back in Winding Creek."

"Then you know Pierce," Buck said. "I'm surprised he never mentioned knowing you."

"No reason he should. Last time I saw him we were in high school, and he moved away before we graduated."

"Yeah. Tough on him and his brothers losing their parents so early. Lucky for them that the Kavanaughs took them in until their uncle moved them to Kansas."

Tough on anyone that young to lose a parent. No one knew that any better than Luke.

"If you're taking care of the horses, who's looking after the critters?" Luke asked.

"Dudley Miles assigned a couple of his cowboys to help out with the herd until Alfred is functioning enough to hire on some new hands. That's how it is in Winding Creek. Neighbors take care of neighbors."

"Certainly seems that way," Luke agreed.

"I'm real sorry about your father's stroke," Buck said. "I didn't really know him very well, but all the same I sure feel bad for him and you."

"I appreciate that."

"I heard a dog barking when I came up. Is that Alfred's dog?"

"Nope. You probably heard Marley. He belongs to one of the cowboys who's working the critters. He brings him with him some days."

"That's a nice-looking horse you're riding," Luke said.

"Yep. Wish Lucky was mine. She's one hell of a cow pony."

"How many horses does Albert have?"

"Eight quarter horses that he keeps in his new fancy horse barn. Those are his pride and joy. Gonna be tough on your dad if he can't ride anymore."

"Hopefully that won't be the case."

"He also has three other cow ponies and one good cutter. They have stalls at the back of the old barn when they're not loose in the pasture."

"What's the size of the cattle herd?"

"I don't have the exact numbers, but I s'pect your dad has a hundred or so Black Angus and damn near that many Santa Gertrudis. That's just an estimate. Numbers change, of course, depending on when he takes the beef to market and how many calves are born in the spring."

"That sounds like a lot of work for a man who's almost seventy to manage," Luke said.

"He always kept a few hired hands around until he got mad about something and ran them off. He had two hired hands when he had the stroke. They weren't from around here. Just showed up from somewhere in Oklahoma around Thanksgiving looking for work. They disappeared when Albert had his stroke and wasn't around to pay them."

Luke couldn't really blame them for that. He couldn't imagine Albert had done anything to deserve a lot of loyalty from them.

He and Buck talked for a few minutes more, long enough to convince Luke that the ranch was not as neglected as the house.

He waited until Buck rode away before stepping inside. Déjà vu hit with a wallop. Memories, both bad and good, came crashing down on him.

It got worse when he reached the kitchen. He leaned against the counter and would have sworn he could smell frying chicken. His mother's shiny black hair would dance about her shoulders as she cooked and she'd be humming the latest hit from the pop chart. Her lips would shimmer with a bright shade of lipstick.

Before everything had gone bad. So many, many years ago.

Luke shut down the recollections before the bittersweet turned to just plain bitter. It was after three in the afternoon, and darkness set in early in January.

From all accounts, his father was being well cared for and might even be asleep for the night before Luke could make the drive to San Antonio, where he was recovering. A visit with him could wait until tomorrow.

Luke would spend the last of the daylight hours checking out the ranch by horseback.

Suddenly he found himself downright eager to get back in the saddle again. Or maybe he was just glad of an excuse to avoid seeing Alfred for one more day.

Chapter Three

Rachel shrugged out of her navy blue blazer and draped it over the arm of the comfortable wing chair before taking a seat in her psychologist's office. Her first visits to Dr. Stephen Lindquist's had been awkward and strained and had always ended with her in tears.

That had been in late September, during the first weeks after she'd been rescued by her sister, Sydney, and Sydney's now husband, Tucker Lawrence. Rachel had been a total wreck then, the panic attacks hitting with excessive regularity and crippling ferocity.

Work was impossible. Sleep deprivation was taking its toll.

Not atypical with her degree of post-traumatic stress, Dr. Lindquist had assured her. His skill and easy manner had quickly won her over, yet she wasn't making the kind of progress she'd hoped for.

She couldn't bring herself to talk about her experience in captivity. Couldn't deal with the fact that if her sister and Tucker had come moments later she would have been burned alive.

Talking or thinking about it brought it all back to life.

Dr. Lindquist settled in his rustic-brown leather chair. "Good to see you, Rachel."

"Thanks for fitting me in on a Friday afternoon with such short notice," she said.

"You sounded a bit panicky on the phone."

"I was. I am." She clasped her hands in her lap. "I had a major meltdown at work this morning." Her voice cracked. She wrapped her arms around her chest as if that could calm her shattered nerves.

"Take a few deep breaths," Dr. Lindquist suggested. "There's no rush. You're my last appointment for the day. You have me as long as you need me."

"Thanks, but you may be sorry you offered that."

"I won't be. Is it the nightmares again?"

"No, though I still have them from time to time. It's just that every time I seem to be getting in control of my fears, something happens to send me back into the self-destruction spiral."

"You're dealing with a lot. A little backsliding is to be expected. We've talked about that."

"I know. But this is more than a little backsliding. I may have blown my career."

The doctor crossed an ankle over his knee. "Why don't you tell me what happened from the beginning?"

"I suppose you've heard that Senator Covey's son, Hayden, has been arrested."

"No way to miss it. The murder of his ex-girlfriend is dominating the news. I'm sure the senator and his wife are devastated."

"And desperate. I didn't know it until this morning, but the senator is a good friend of my boss, Eric Fitch Sr."

"Guess that means your firm will be defending Hayden."

"It looks that way. I was offered the chance to be the lead attorney in charge of his defense."

"How do you feel about that?"

"Troubled. Confused. Anxious." Her muscles tightened and she felt a nagging ache at her right temple.

"It's the kind of high-profile case that can make or break a defense attorney," she continued, "the kind of opportunity I've been waiting for. The kind I thought I was ready for."

"And now you're not sure. What changed your mind?"

"Doubts that I can handle the job. Thoughts that I don't want to handle the job."

He leaned in closer. "Go on."

"Senator and Mrs. Covey brought their son into the office this morning for a preliminary interview. As I shook hands with Hayden, I stared into the cold, barren intensity of his predatory eyes and an icy shiver ran though me. In that second, it was as if I knew that he was capable of murder.

"No evidence had been presented. It was nothing Hayden had said or done. I just looked into his eyes and saw Roy Sales."

"What did you do?"

"I mumbled something about feeling ill, which I was, and then stood and staggered out of the meeting."

Rachel covered her eyes with her hands, fighting back salty tears of frustration. Her life had changed forever. Now the past was destroying her career with no relief in sight.

"If it turns out Hayden Covey is guilty of the brutal murder of his former girlfriend, I'd say your assessment of him is right on target," the doctor said.

"Which doesn't excuse my unprofessional behavior."

"Have you talked to your boss about the incident?"

"Not yet. I think he was with the Coveys the rest of the morning, but I'm sure it's just a matter of time until he confronts me about my reaction. I'll be lucky if I'm not fired. My boss put me to the test and I failed miserably."

"*Failure* is a strong word."

"And not one I'm used to," she admitted. "But nothing is what I'm used to anymore and I'm tired of having my friends and coworkers feel sorry for me instead of seeing me as an equal."

"I'm sure most of them mean well," Dr. Lindquist said.

"I know, but it's not the way I want to live."

"Maybe it's time you changed your life. Go somewhere where everyone doesn't know about your past."

"You're starting to sound like my sister, Dr. Lindquist, and I get her advice for free."

"What kind of advice does she give you?"

"Stop putting so much pressure on myself. She thinks I should quit the firm and spend some time finding myself again—away from the world of defending people accused of violent crimes."

"How do you feel about that?"

"You know, Doctor, sometimes I wish you'd just give me answers instead of trying to lead me to work my way through the impossible maze."

An unexpected smile touched the doctor's lips. "Sometimes I wish I could, too. Unfortunately, that's not the way this works. The real answers must come from you.

"So, back to the question. How do you feel about Sydney's suggestion that you take a less stressful job for a while, maybe a change of scenery, as well?"

"It feels like I'd be giving up. It feels like I would have lost and Roy Sales has won."

"Any other considerations?"

As usual, she had the feeling Dr. Lindquist was seeing right through her. "There are times I long to walk away from it all," she admitted reluctantly. "But working for a prominent law firm was the dream that got me through law school. So much time and work have been invested into that dream. I can't just throw that away."

"Sometimes dreams change."

"Or they can be changed for you."

"Have you considered other career options?"

"Not exactly, but I have a friend who specializes in working with charitable organizations—handles lawsuits and tax issues for them and works with people who wish to set up foundations or donate money in their wills. She loves it. Says she always feels like she's on the right side."

"That has a lot of plusses?" the doctor said.

"Then is just walking away from my job what you think I should do?"

"It's what you think you should do that matters, Rachel. I don't see that as giving up. Sometimes changing life paths is the most difficult decision of all."

"I never looked at it that way."

"You're a tough, smart woman with good instincts. You'll make the right decision for you. It just takes time."

"You have more confidence in me than I do in myself."

"You'll get there. I am puzzled, though, why Eric Sr. didn't just take the lead on this case himself."

"He's concerned his friendship with the senator might bias the jury against him. And he claims that I'd be more effective at convincing the jury of Hayden's innocence."

"Because of your own past? Your opinion of Hayden Covey would likely count for a lot, considering what you've been through."

She thought painstakingly about Dr. Lindquist's comment and then cringed as the truth about Eric's more likely motives took root. He didn't think she was the most capable defense attorney at the firm.

He was using her, putting his faith in the jurors pitying her and believing she'd never defend Hayden unless she fully believed in his innocence.

Her insides twisted. She had no proof of the theory, but it made sense. How had she not seen that before?

By the time the session with Dr. Lindquist was finished and she reached her car, her decision had been made.

If she hurried, she could catch the most senior partner before he left the office.

She couldn't go on being a victim forever. She had to fight back.

Chapter Four

A light rain dotted her windshield as Rachel exited the multilevel parking garage at her firm and started toward home. Her emotions still on a roller coaster, the ringing of her phone startled her.

She checked the caller ID on the hands-free display. Her sister, Sydney. She took the call, though she'd hoped not to share her big announcement with her sister until she'd gotten used to it herself.

"Good evening, Sydney. How's the world inside the FBI this Friday night?"

"Urgent and crisis-filled, as usual, though I plan not to think about that his weekend. I'm only a few miles from Winding Creek now. I'll be there for dinner with Esther and the rest of the family. When are you arriving?"

When was she arriving? Oh, God. "This is the weekend of Grace's baby shower, isn't it?"

"Don't tell me you forgot, Rachel."

"Okay. I won't tell you. When is the shower?"

"Tomorrow afternoon at three. It's at Dani's Delights. Dani is closing the bakery early for the party. It's a really big deal. Half the women in town are coming. Everybody loves Grace."

"Me included," Rachel said, "but…"

"She'll be very disappointed if you're not here. Besides, you and I haven't gotten together since Christmas. I'm really looking forward to seeing you."

"Yeah. I'd like to see you, too," she admitted, suddenly realizing just how much. "I'll start out early in the morning. I'm far too tired to make that drive tonight."

"Super, though I was hoping you'd taken the afternoon off and were coming in tonight so we could have one of our all-talk and no-sleep slumber parties the way we used to."

"You mean back before you had a gorgeous husband to keep you entertained at night?"

"Right. But he's competing in a rodeo in Longview tonight and tomorrow morning, so he won't make it here until late tomorrow afternoon. The good news is we're both taking Monday and Tuesday off."

"So I'm second choice?"

"Yep. But I just checked the radar and it shows a line of thundershowers moving into the area over the next few hours, so it's just as well you're not driving this way now."

"I do hate driving in the rain."

"You did forget, though. I mean, there's nothing going on there that made you have second thoughts about coming?"

Sydney never took things at face value. It was all that FBI training, Rachel expected. But her insight hit too close to home far too often.

"What are you intimating, my crime-fighting sister?"

"Just wondering if it's the thought of returning to Winding Creek that's really bothering you."

"No," she lied. "I'm fine with Winding Creek."

"Then promise you're not going to make some new excuse to get out of coming tomorrow so you can stay home and work. You need a break."

Yes, she did. She hadn't intended to just blurt out her news, but there was no real reason to keep it a secret.

"I know you're sitting down, since you're driving," Rachel said, "but prepare yourself for a shock."

"You've met a man?"

"Gads. That's the last thing I need."

"A matter of opinion. Then what is it?"

"I will no longer be overworking. As of about thirty minutes ago, I don't have a job or a career. I did make off with a few company pens, though, as I stormed out of the building."

"You got fired?"

"No. I beat old Fitch to it. I quit."

"You're joking."

"Nope. In fact, I may be as shocked as you that I quit, but it felt right. Still does. But also a bit scary."

"I can't wait to hear all the details. But let me just say, I'm in favor of the decision. And you haven't lost a career permanently. You're still a dynamite attorney. You'll land on your feet somewhere where they don't expect you to give up sleep permanently in exchange for billable hours."

"I hope you're right. We'll talk more when I get there."

"Now I really can't wait to see you. Actually, the whole family will be thrilled to see you again. Esther asks about you every time we talk."

Esther was a jewel. So were all three of the Lawrence brothers and their families who had come home to Winding Creek and to Esther Kavanaugh.

The only problem was that the warm and loving family members were Sydney's in-laws—not Rachel's.

"Don't mention my quitting my job to anyone else just yet."

"I'll have to tell Tucker. We talk about everything, but I'll tell him to keep it under his hat."

Rachel's new life was off and running—ready or not.

RACHEL KEPT HER eyes on the passing scenery, watching for the gate to the Double K Ranch. All things considered, she was feeling surprisingly upbeat, or at least several notches above gloom.

Perhaps the reality that she was unemployed for the first time since she'd graduated from law school hadn't fully sunk in. Or maybe Sydney was right about her needing a mental, emotional and physical break from the stress that Fitch, Fitch and Baumer provided.

The sun claimed dominance over a few cumulus clouds. Michael Bublé was crooning on her car's radio. And she was actually going to spend two full days with her sister instead of driving back home on Sunday morning to a crush of paperwork.

She basically had nothing on her plate in the foreseeable future except freedom and possibly a few hours doing wrap-up at the office. She'd offered two weeks' notice. A shocked and irritated Eric Fitch Sr. had said that wasn't necessary.

All he needed was a verbal agreement that she would answer any questions that might arise concerning cases she'd been involved with. Eric Fitch Jr. had come by while she was collecting her personal belongings and tried to talk her into staying, assuring her he'd cleared the offer with his dad.

He'd offered a raise. She'd been tempted, but not enough to stay.

Lost in her thoughts again, she almost missed the

Double K's metal gate and had to throw on her brakes to keep from passing it by. She made the turn too fast, skidding across a wet patch of grass that bordered the ranch road.

She slowed and stopped at the closed and latched gate. Esther had talked about putting in an automatic gate opener to save herself having to get out in the weather. Obviously that was still on her to-do list. Neither weather nor much else slowed down Esther Kavanaugh.

Rachel switched the gear to Park but kept the motor running. She'd opened the door and was about to climb from behind the wheel when she was startled by the clattering engine noise of another vehicle.

She checked the rearview mirror. An old, mud-encrusted pickup truck had made the turn and had followed her to the gate. The male driver stopped mere inches behind her, blocking her between his front bumper and the closed gate.

She jerked her door closed and pushed the lock button. Her heart pounded against the walls of her chest. Her lungs burned. Her stomach churned sickeningly.

The driver got out of his truck and started toward her. She switched the gear to Drive and poised her foot on the accelerator. If he so much as touched her car, she would ram through the gate, knocking it from its hinges. She wouldn't stop until she reached Esther's house.

As the man neared, he smiled and tipped his gray Stetson. Nothing about him looked dangerous. His smile was anything but threatening. Telling herself that only barely eased her surge of apprehension.

She clutched the steering wheel so tight her knuckles turned white.

The cowboy sauntered past her locked door, walked to the front of her car and unlatched the gate. He was opening the door for her. She took a deep breath and let her fingers relax their hold on the steering wheel.

The gate swung open and the cowboy motioned her through—an extremely good-looking cowboy, though she hadn't noticed that before. She lowered her window and waved as she drove past him.

Her pulse was back to near normal by the time she reached the rambling ranch house. The sight of Esther's house had a further calming effect on her.

Colorful pillows adorned the wide porch swing. Painted rocking chairs were pulled up to a round table topped with a pot of colorful pansies. A clump of sweet alyssum huddled next to the steps. Winter jasmine climbed the railings on the north end of the porch.

Rachel parked in the gravel drive on the far side

of the house, a recent addition that kept visitors from dodging mud holes on mornings such as this.

Once more, the cowboy parked behind her. This time she waited for him to get out of the truck. The unwarranted panic attack had passed.

"Thanks for handling the gate chores," she said.

"My pleasure." He pointed to his worn Western boots. "Those high-heeled fancy boots you're wearing don't look like they'd take too well to mud. These goat-ropers are made for chunking through whatever they face."

"Goat-roper?"

"Just a term. I don't really rope goats in them— not that I couldn't."

"I'll bet."

He extended his hand. "Luke Dawkins. The prodigal son of Alfred Dawkins, returning to Winding Creek for duty."

She slid her hand into his much larger one. An unexpected wave of awareness zinged through her. That frightened her almost as much as her initial reaction to him had. "Rachel Maxwell. I'm Sydney Lawrence's sister, just visiting—no duty."

She waited for the look of pity that frequently followed the act of telling anyone her name. There was none. Evidently he didn't know of her past. The chances were slim to none she could keep it that way.

They started up the wide wooden steps to the porch together. Their arms brushed. Her first impulse was to pull away from him. She didn't.

Before she had time to ring the bell, the door opened and Sydney appeared, with Esther a step behind. "You made it," Esther said.

Sidney spotted Luke and looked shocked. "And you bought a guest."

"Not intentionally," Luke said. "I'm just a stray who followed her home. Luke Dawkins."

"A prodigal son," Rachel offered to fill a sudden, awkward silence on Sydney's part.

"Well, of course you are," Esther said, pushing to the front. "You haven't changed a bit, Luke, except for that facial hair. Just threw me off that you arrived with our Rachel."

"What can I say? When a beautiful woman shows up, I don't argue with fate."

"You're in your dad's truck," Esther said, leaning over to look past them. "Hope that's not all you have to get around in. To hear Alfred tell it, it only runs half the time."

"I was afraid it wouldn't make it here," Luke admitted. "But I have my own truck back at the ranch, so if this one makes it back home, I'll park it and leave it until I can get it tuned up."

Luke touched a hand to the small of Rachel's back as they stepped inside.

Once again, her nerves zinged.

It couldn't get any crazier than this.

Chapter Five

Luke's ego took a blow. He was definitely the odd man out where the two sisters were concerned. They were both talking at once, the topics changing as fast as if this were a game-show lightning round. He didn't even try to keep up.

Within ten minutes Sydney and Rachel excused themselves to go wrap gifts for an afternoon baby shower. Luke watched Rachel walk away. She was hot as a bonfire and there was no gold band on her ring finger.

If he were planning to stick around awhile, he'd hit on her big-time, though she was probably miles out of his league. But as soon as he figured out what to do about his father and the Arrowhead Hills Ranch, he was out of here.

Unless Alfred kicked him out sooner.

"It's good to have you here in my house again after so many years," Esther said once they were alone.

"You've grown into a fine-looking young man. Your mother would have been mighty proud of you."

"Thanks. Being here reminds me of her."

"She was a very special woman, one of the best friends I've had in my life, even though she was a couple of decades younger and had four times the energy I did. I miss her to this day, but it's probably not the best time for going all syrupy. I know you're here to talk about Alfred's problems."

"I am," he agreed. "I still don't know much more than what you told me on the phone. The rehab center is not big on giving out information other than what's on his chart. Assisted shower at eight. Occupational therapy scheduled for one. That and other equally unhelpful info."

"Did you talk to the medical supervisor where he's staying or the doctor who cared for him in the hospital?"

"I've talked to both with equally worthless results. The doctor quoted some medical jargon to describe the stroke and possible causes but didn't give me anything definite on the prognosis. He insisted there was no way to be certain at this point if or how long Alfred would need permanent care. I'm supposed to meet with the medical supervisor this afternoon."

"You're driving to San Antonio today?"

"Yep. I need to see his condition for myself and at least let him know I'm here for him—if he cares."

"I visited him again Wednesday," Esther said. "He's throwing a fit to go home, but he can't get around well enough to take care of himself. He definitely can't handle cooking chores or bathing and shaving."

"Then you think he'll need someone with him twenty-four hours a day?"

"At least at first, and I predict he'll go through the ceiling if you suggest he go anywhere when he leaves the rehab facility except back to the ranch."

"A ranch he can't take care of on his own. He'll have to hire someone to manage everything, and unless he's changed a lot in eleven years, he's not good at delegating authority." Luke couldn't see any way this was going to turn out well.

"I have a fresh pot of coffee in the kitchen," Esther said. "Will you have a cup with me?"

"Sure." He needed a beer more, but it was still morning and he had a visit with Alfred staring him in the face, so he'd stick with the caffeine.

He followed her to the kitchen.

"Cream or sugar?"

"Just black, thanks."

She filled two mugs and set them on the small table in the kitchen breakfast nook. He held her chair and then took a seat across from her.

Esther sipped her brew. "I've probably depressed

you enough, but do you have any other questions that I might be able to answer?"

"How was Alfred's health before the stroke?"

"He was slowing down a bit, only sixty-nine, but looked older than he was. Not much meat on his bones. Comes from living alone, and you know how that Texas sun turns your skin to leather if you don't slather on sunscreen every day."

"But he still supervised the running of the ranch and rode his horses."

"Yes, indeed. From what I heard, he'd hardly let anyone else touch his quarter horses. Rumor was he loved them like they were his babies."

Too bad he hadn't felt that way about Luke or his mother.

Esther stared into her cup. "I guess the doctor told you the stroke affected his memory. I reckon it's getting better, though.

"The first time Grace and I drove down to visit him, he had no idea who we were. Went into a rant. Accused us of trying to steal things from his room."

"Now, that sounds like the father I remember."

"I think this was more than attitude. Before I left he was calling Grace and me by name, as if it just suddenly came to him who the heck we were. He settled down after that."

"I ran into Buck Stallings when I arrived at the ranch yesterday. He told me Dad's hired hands disappeared when my father had the stroke and wasn't around to pay them."

"They quit, all right. Just up and rode off without bothering to tell anybody. Pierce thinks they probably made off with enough equipment to make up for any wages they lost."

"Sounds like Alfred owes Pierce and Dudley Miles a great deal for stepping in and taking care of his livestock and horses."

"They aren't expecting any thanks. People around these parts take care of their neighbors when they see a need even if the neighbor is as ornery as Alfred. My Charlie would have been the first one to the rescue if he was still living."

"I'm sure he would. I'm sorry about your loss."

"I appreciate that. You know, I keep thinking I'll miss him less as days go by, but it doesn't work that way. Spend almost half a century of your life with a person and he's as much a part of you as breathing."

Luke's longest relationship to date had lasted just over three months. He couldn't even imagine that many years with the same woman, but he nodded like he got it.

Esther worried the handle of her coffee mug and then took another sip. "You think it's over, but life goes on. Blessings, too." A smile touched her lips and glinted in her eyes. "Never had a family of my own. Now I'm overrun with kids and grandkids that I couldn't love more if they were flesh and blood."

"You seem happy."

"If I felt any better, I'd drop my harp plumb through the clouds." She pushed her cup away. "And here I go rambling on about my good fortune with you here to talk about your poor father."

"I was just thinking that if Dad didn't recognize you, it's definitely not likely he'll recognize me."

"No way of knowing. How long has it been since you were last here in Winding Creek?"

"Going on twelve years."

"But you've surely talked since then?"

"I call at Christmas and Father's Day when I'm somewhere I can. The conversations are strained, awkward and short. We didn't talk a lot more when we lived together unless he was barking orders."

Esther reached across the table and laid a blue-veined and wrinkled hand on his. "I know you two have had a rocky relationship and it's mostly his doing. But he needs you, Luke. You're the only family he's got, and let's face it, he's better at making enemies than friends."

Dread ground in the pit of Luke's stomach. He'd arrived at Esther's this morning holding out a little hope that things weren't as bad as he feared. Now he figured they were worse and there was no easy fix in sight.

"Guess I'd better get going if I'm going to see Dad before I talk to the medical supervisor. I have a few more chores I want to get done at the ranch before I leave."

He finished off the rest of his coffee, stood and carried his cup to the sink.

Esther followed him. "I'll be gone to Grace's baby shower this afternoon, but I'll be home tonight or after church tomorrow if you want to discuss what comes next with Alfred or just blow off a little frustration."

"I may take you up on that, and I appreciate all you and the other neighbors have done."

"Even better, why don't you join us for dinner tonight, Luke? It's a night off from kitchen duties for the women, since we're throwing the baby shower for Pierce's wife, Grace, but Pierce and Riley are grilling."

"Riley Lawrence?"

"Yes. Pierce, Riley and Tucker Lawrence. I figured you'd remember them."

"I remember that you and Charlie took them in for nearly a year after their parents were killed in the car crash."

Luke had been envious of the brothers, had wished the Kavanaughs had taken him in after his mother died instead of leaving him to take the brunt of his dad's verbal abuse and mean disposition.

Luke twirled the strong black brew in his mug and then sipped. "Sounds like a family reunion."

"I guess it is, of sorts, except that two of the Lawrence brothers are happily married and living in Winding Creek now. Tucker and Sydney have an apartment in Dallas, but with his rodeoing and Sydney's work as an FBI agent, I think they call this home as much as anywhere else."

"Whatever works."

"That's what I say, too," Esther agreed. "Come to dinner tonight and the guys can catch you up on all their news."

"I'd love to see them if you're sure I won't be intruding."

"There's always room for one more at my old dining room table. How about you, Luke? Are you married?"

"Nope. Never even came close and plan to keep it that way."

She smiled and he could swear he saw a conspiratorial gleam in her eye.

"Seems like I remember Pierce, Riley and Tucker saying that exact same thing not too long ago."

He stood to go. "Stay here," he said. "I can let myself out."

"We'll be looking for you tonight. Come hungry."

"I'm always hungry."

When he reached the short hallway, he heard

voices and recognized Rachel's at once. An unexpected surge of pleasure overrode some of the anxiety about dealing with his father.

A decent meal and a visit with the Lawrence brothers would be nice, but it was the thought of seeing Rachel again that really cranked up his anticipation.

SYDNEY LAWRENCE LOOKED up from the fingernail she was applying a mending touch of red polish to as Rachel swept into the room. "Holy Smoly, do you look hot!"

Rachel did a quick twirl in the full-skirted, jewel-toned dress and then struck a sexy pose. "Is it too dressy for an afternoon party?"

"It's perfect. I love the cutout at the neck."

"Not too much cleavage?"

"Heavens, no. Barely a hint. Love those strappy heels, too."

"It was either this or one of the depressing navy or gray suits I wear to work. Oops. I *used* to wear to work."

"I have to say you're taking your newly unemployed status well. I was afraid you'd be in the dumps and not even show."

"I'm not sure the full reality of my situation has hit me yet."

"Or maybe it has and that's why you're glowing."

"No. That's the new blush I picked up at Macy's

last week. Dusty Fire. Guaranteed to set me apart from the crowd."

"From the way hunky Luke Dawkins was looking at you today, I'd say it's surpassing promised expectations."

"He was just being nice and making conversation."

"Really? Because it sure seemed like there was a sizzle between you two when I met you at the door."

"Don't even go there. My life is too screwed up right now to even notice a man."

But Sydney knew she had noticed. The rosy color creeping into her cheeks right now was proof of that. A casual flirtation might do Rachel good, but Sydney doubted she was emotionally ready for anything more.

Rachel sat on the edge of the bed amid the wrapped packages. "Is Esther going to ride into town with us?" she asked, no doubt ready to direct the conversation away from Luke.

"No, Pierce is going to drive Grace and Esther to the bakery and he'll pick up Dani's daughter, Constance, and bring her back here to play with his daughter, Jaci, while we party."

"Dad in charge. Everything around here really is a family affair," Rachel said.

"I know and I love it. Do you still want to keep the fact that you quit your job a secret from the rest of the family?"

"For now. This is Grace's special weekend. I don't want it to turn into a whine party for me."

"I haven't even had a chance to tell Tucker yet."

"When are you expecting him?"

"He called a few minutes ago. He's about an hour out, so he'll be at the ranch by the time we get back from the party."

"And then you'll forget the rest of us exist."

"True." Which was exactly why she should tackle the bad news she had for Rachel now.

She couldn't bring herself to do it. This was the most relaxed she'd seen Rachel since she'd lived through hell. She couldn't bring herself to spoil the moment. Tomorrow would be soon enough to drag her back into the Roy Sales hell.

ODDS WERE AGAINST Rachel feeling at home at a baby shower in Winding Creek. Everyone in town knew of her terrifying past.

The saving grace was that since they knew the intimate details, no one ever mentioned it to her.

There would be no endless questions the way there often were when she met someone new. No staring at her as if the experience made her less human now. No more expressions of pity that made Rachel feel worse instead of better about herself.

She and Sydney grabbed the gifts from the back

of Sydney's car and joined the stream of chatting and laughing local women pouring into Dani's Delights.

Rachel set the wrapped baby carrier on the floor next to a long table that was already overflowing with presents. A squeal captured her attention just as Dani and Riley Lawrence's eleven-year-old newly adopted daughter threw her arms around Rachel's waist.

"Yay. You came. You can go riding with us tomorrow. We have two new horses. And I'm learning to be a barrel rider. I can show you."

Words spilled out of Constance's mouth so fast, Rachel could barely follow her train of thought. Constance's excitement was contagious, exactly what Rachel needed to keep her in the here and now. "I'm staying all day tomorrow and I brought my riding clothes. And I definitely want a barrel riding exhibition."

"I'm pretty good. One day I want to be in the rodeo like Uncle Tucker."

"Now, that sounds exciting. When you are, I'll be in the stands cheering for you."

"Yes, but my parents say I still have to study hard at school even if horses don't care if I know about geography and math. I hate math, especially word problems."

Dani appeared at her daughter's side, opened her arms and welcomed Rachel with a warm hug. "I'm so glad you could make it. By the way, you look terrific. I need to absorb some of your fashion savvy."

"You're the most popular woman in town in your chocolate- and flour-smeared white apron. If I were you, I wouldn't change a thing."

They laughed and then all attention turned to the front door as the guest of honor arrived, accompanied by Esther, Pierce and his daughter, Jaci.

The baby bump was no longer just a bump. Grace was due in a matter of weeks and, with her petite frame, she looked to be all baby.

Nonetheless, she was as beautiful as ever and Pierce helped her to the chair situated beneath a colorful balloon arch as if she was the most fragile and cherished treasure on earth.

Someone pushed a crystal flute of sparkling champagne into Rachel's hand. The bell around the door dinged as another group of laughing ladies entered. The party had begun and surprisingly the celebratory spirit overtook even Rachel.

Grace sounded positively joyous and yet she'd once lived in a hellish nightmare, too. Rachel wondered if she'd ever find the kind of happiness Grace enjoyed.

Could she let herself?

Luke Dawkins drove the forty-five minutes to the rehab center on the outskirts of San Antonio where his dad was receiving his care. He arrived at approximately half past two for a three o'clock appointment with the medical supervisor.

The L-shaped building was redbrick, set in a park-like setting with several bare-branched oak trees and a few pines shading benches and small, gurgling fountains.

Not the worst of places to be housed if you needed care, but definitely not the wide-open spaces of Arrowhead Hills.

There was a covered drop-off area at the front door. A sign directed him to a visitor parking lot in the rear. A couple of dozen cars and trucks and two vans emblazoned with the name of the center were parked near the back entrance.

Luke climbed out of his truck and locked it before sauntering up the narrow walk to the back door. He hesitated before opening the door, gearing himself to deal with whatever came next.

His father had been fifty-eight when Luke cut out. A big man, over six feet tall, muscles developed from a lifetime of hard work. Rigid. Hardheaded. His way or the highway.

But Luke himself had changed a lot in eleven years and not just physically. He was less impulsive, more prone to think before acting. Maybe time or aging and the stroke had mellowed Alfred.

He stopped at the nurses' station at the end of a

short hallway. One nurse was at her computer. Another was on the phone. What he guessed was an aide pushed a patient in a wheelchair down the hall as Luke waited for one of the nurses to acknowledge him.

The man in the wheelchair waved and smiled—a dead giveaway it wasn't Alfred.

Nurse number two, a middle-aged brunette with short hair and extremely red lipstick, hung up her phone and asked if she could help him. Her name tag said she was an RN named Louise.

"I'm Alfred Dawkins's son. I have an appointment."

Louise clapped her hands together softly as a smile lit up her face. "You must be Luke. We've been hoping a family member would show up."

"I came as soon as I could and I was assured he was not in critical condition."

"He's fine, but he's a handful to deal with. I'm sure he'll be much easier to handle now that you're here."

"I wouldn't count on that. I also have an appointment with Carolyn Schultz."

"Great. I know she's looking forward to discussing Alfred's progress with you. She's not here yet, but your father is in his room, probably watching TV. I'm sure you're anxious to see him."

Anxious, but not eager. But he could think of no legitimate excuse to put the visit off.

"Alfred is in Room 109, just around the corner. Now, don't get upset if he doesn't recognize you at once. He sometimes gets confused when he has visitors."

"I understand."

"Other times he's clued in and recognizes visitors right away. Either way, he's slow at getting his words out."

"I'll keep my expectations low." That should be easy enough.

He followed the nurse to Alfred's room. She entered before him. Alfred was propped up in a hospital bed, wearing a blue shirt only half-buttoned with food stains down the front. He looked frail and years older than Luke remembered him.

He felt a jolt to his gut. The man in the hospital bed was not the father he remembered.

Louise walked over and stood next to Alfred's bed. "You have a visitor," she announced in a cheery voice.

Alfred grunted and pulled up his sheet before looking at Luke. For the first few seconds, there was nothing in his facial expression to indicate he recognized Luke. Then his thin lips all but disappeared in a scowl.

Louise stood back so that Luke could step in closer. "Do you know who this is?" she asked.

"Hell, yes. But he's...too soon. I'm not...not dead yet."

That was the father he remembered.

Welcome home, Luke Dawkins.

Chapter Six

Luke's emotions had run the gauntlet over the past few hours. His nerves had skidded along for the maddening ride from concern to fuming to disgruntled exasperation. By the time he stopped behind a row of three pickup trucks at the Kavanaugh house, he was slowly inching toward reason.

His dad hadn't sent for him and clearly didn't want him around. The easiest and likely the smartest thing Luke could do right now was clear out. Let his dad hire someone to run his own damn ranch any way he liked or let it go to weed and empty pastures if that was the way hardheaded Alfred Dawkins wanted it.

But Luke had never looked for the easy way out or shirked responsibility—which left him stuck neck-deep in the dilemma of where to go from here.

He struggled to rein in his conflicting emotions as he reached Esther's wide front porch. He put his hand on the doorbell but didn't push.

Coming here was a mistake. There was no way

he'd be decent dinner company tonight. Besides, judging from the trucks parked out front, he was likely late.

Before he could cut and run, the door opened and Rachel Maxwell greeted him with a melodic hello that softened the edges of his lousy mood like magic.

Her voice wasn't the half of it. She'd been a knockout this morning in her jeans and cotton shirt. All fancied up, she was luscious.

It wasn't the dress so much as the way she wore it. The soft fabric hugged her perfect breasts and then tightened at her tiny waist before billowing out over her shapely hips.

The skirt stopped a few inches above the knees, highlighting her dynamite calves and the straps on a pair of nosebleed heels that wrapped around her slender ankles.

When she smiled and looked at him with those gold-specked, dusky eyes, he turned away to keep from melting. He had to pull his gaze away from her before he could speak.

"I didn't know we were playing dress-up. I'd have come with my boots shined and my jeans creased," he said, determined to keep the tone light.

She laughed and motioned him inside. "You'll fit in perfectly. Normally I'd be in jeans myself, but I decided to go for the girly look at Grace's baby shower this afternoon."

"You aced it."

"Thank you, I guess."

"Is this the Grace who's married to Pierce Lawrence?"

"Yes. Have you met her?"

"Haven't had the pleasure."

"You'll love her, guaranteed. She went home to rest awhile, but she'll be back for dinner."

"Then I must be too early. I'm not crashing," he teased. "I was actually invited by Esther, but she didn't mention a time."

"The guys are doing the cooking chores tonight You can never tie them down to a time. They tend to grill for hours."

"Ranchers need their beef and plenty of it," Luke said.

"So it seems. I'm a city girl myself. Sushi and a salad are my usual Saturday night splurge."

"I'm going to pretend I didn't hear you say that."

"Does that mean you're a cowboy, too?"

"I am this week."

"There must be a story there."

"Not one you'd want to hear before dinner—or after, either, for that matter."

"Now you've really piqued my curiosity. Do you know all three of the Lawrence brothers?"

"We went to school together many years ago."

"Pierce and Riley are in the backyard slaving over

the hot charcoal. They may put you to work if you venture that way, but I'm sure they'd love to see you again and say hello."

"Sounds like a good idea."

"Then follow me."

The view was almost as spectacular from the rear. Hard to imagine he could feel anything sensual after the visit he'd had with his father, but maybe it was his survival instincts kicking in. Or perhaps the fact that he hadn't been with a woman in more months than he could count on his fingers and toes.

More likely it was simply that she was a natural temptress.

They walked through the house, onto the covered back porch and down the few steps to the yard. Mouthwatering odors spilled from a huge barrel-shaped grill.

They walked closer and watched as Riley basted a slab of ribs with one hand. The fingers of the other hand were wrapped around a beer.

Pierce stepped over to greet them. "Glad you could make it, Luke. Esther said she twisted your arm to accept her dinner invitation."

"Actually, she just said 'food' and I jumped at the chance."

"As you can see, we have enough meat here to clog the arteries of a dozen more guys," Riley said.

"Don't bet on it. My arteries haven't seen a Texas meal like this in recent memory."

Pierce turned to Riley. "You remember Luke Dawkins, don't you?"

"I do." Riley set his beer down on the worktable and extended a hand to Luke. "It's been a while."

"Yes, it has. A lot of water under the bridge since those high school days."

"I remember you had a mean fastball," Pierce said. "Best southpaw to ever come out of the Hill Country, the newspapers used to brag. Did you ever go pro?"

"No. I knocked around in the Northwest for a few months and then joined the marines. Got to see the world—well, at least the stony cliffs of Afghanistan from an Apache helicopter."

"I'd like to hear about that one day," Pierce said.

"It was interesting," Luke admitted. "But get me started and you've wasted an evening."

"Sorry about your father," Riley said. "Have you seen him yet?"

"Today."

"How'd that go?" Pierce asked.

"It could have been worse. He could have shot me. Luckily he wasn't toting."

"Sounds like the stroke didn't affect his disposition," Riley joked.

"Not for the better," Luke said. "And that is a subject best discussed when we don't want to lose our appetites. What can I do to help with dinner? I'm great at opening cans or poking meat with a fork."

"Thanks for the offer, but we've got it covered," Pierce said. "I would suggest you and Rachel take a walk and get out of this smoke, except if she were to fall in those shoes, the height could cause major injuries."

Rachel's hands flew to her hips, but the sparkle in her eyes proved it was a show of fake indignation. "You don't like my shoes?"

"I love your shoes," Pierce said, "just not for walking."

"Walking is overrated," Riley said. "Beer, on the other hand…"

He reached into a cooler and pulled out two bottles of an amber brew. He opened them both and handed one to Rachel and one to Luke. "Now, you two find a less smoky spot and get better acquainted while I try to keep Pierce from burning his brisket."

"Don't you worry about my brisket, bro. You just take care of your ribs."

"I think that's our cue to get out of the way of the cooks," Rachel said. "Esther is resting from the day's activities, and I don't want to venture into what Sydney and Tucker might be doing after spending two weeks apart. But I'm pretty sure I can make it as far as the front porch in these shoes."

"I'll drink to that." Luke clinked his bottle with Rachel's. It was the best invitation he'd had in years.

THE LAST RAYS of the setting sun were shooting golden streaks across the sky as Luke and Rachel settled on the porch swing. The afternoon had been unusually warm for January, but a breeze stirred now and the temperatures were dropping.

Rachel shivered and wrapped her arms around her chest.

Without a word, Luke shrugged out of his denim jacket and cloaked it around her shoulders. His hands brushed her neck as he did, creating a startling tingle. There was no reasonable explanation for the way his nearness affected her.

"Now you'll be cold," she said. "I can step inside and get a wrap."

"What do you think I am, a wimp? Besides, the jacket looks far better on you. Adds a certain Texas flair to those daring shoes."

They both laughed and she realized that she actually felt at ease with him. That, paired with quitting her job, was probably a sign she was totally losing it.

Luke used his foot to move the swing in a slow, rhythmic motion. "Great family you have, Rachel Maxwell."

"They're not exactly my family, but they make me feel as if I am. I always feel at home here."

"I get that. As a kid, I loved coming here with my mother. There were always cookies and laughter and lots of times Charlie would play catcher while I worked on my fastball."

"Charlie must have been very special. Esther talks about him with such love. So do all the Lawrences."

"This family has grown significantly since my mother was alive. I need a crash course on who goes with whom."

"It's not that difficult. Pierce is married to Grace, who is pregnant and due in a few weeks. You can't confuse her with anyone else. Jaci is Pierce's six-year-old daughter from a previous marriage, but he has custody while her mother is in Cuba with her new husband."

"Got it. And I know Tucker is married to your sister, Sydney, whom I met earlier."

"Right. And Riley is married to Dani, whom you haven't met as yet. She is a fabulous pastry chef and owns Dani's Delights, a bakery and coffee shop on Main Street in Winding Creek."

"Do they have children?"

"They have just completed the adoption process for Dani's orphaned niece, Constance. Constance is only eleven, but she adores Tucker and loves the rodeo. If you stay in town long enough, she'll insist on demonstrating her barrel riding skills for you."

"How did Tucker and Sydney meet?"

And this was where the fun began. Rachel's chest tightened. She sipped her beer as she considered her answer.

"Sydney was in Winding Creek working an investigation and Tucker was here visiting Esther and his brothers. They met and that was it. Bells ringing, birds singing, butterflies fluttering. Just like in the movies."

"Then you believe in love at first sight?"

"For them. Not for everyone." She shifted in the swing, turning toward Luke. His rugged masculinity was daunting, yet enticing.

She'd never been particularly fond of facial hair, but his was incredibly sexy. Close-trimmed, little more than a five-o'clock shadow. She imagined how the trendy strip of hair above his mouth would tickle if they were to kiss.

Which they weren't going to do.

"Tell me about yourself, Luke Dawkins," she said, determined to change the subject before they entered forbidden territory.

"Not a lot to tell," Luke said.

"You said you're only a cowboy this week? Does that mean you're not a die-hard rancher like Pierce, Riley and Tucker?"

"I thought I might be at one time. That life didn't happen for me, so I took another path."

"And became a marine?"

"Eventually. That's a lifestyle all its own, though the guys in my squad did nickname me Maverick."

"It could be the saunter," Rachel said. "You authentic Texas cowboys have that down to a fine art. And you still have a bit of that Texas drawl."

"Is that a bad thing?"

"Apparently not where women are concerned. Cowboys are the in thing these days. Just check out the covers of the romance novels on the shelves in your favorite bookstore."

"I'll make it a point to do that," he said, exaggerating his drawl for emphasis.

"How long have you been a civilian again?"

"Only three months."

"Has it been hard adjusting to your new life?"

"Much more difficult than I expected. Who knew it would be so hard to find a satisfactory replacement for combat?"

"Have you?"

"No, but I can tell you what doesn't work for me. Sitting at a desk all day. Bureaucracy and all the red tape that holds it together. Politics—at any level."

"So now you've come back to your roots."

"Not by choice. My dad had a stroke and I'm the only family he has, not that we have much of a relationship."

"Why is that?"

"He kicked me out of the house when I was eighteen and has pretty much cut me out of his life since then. That tends to cause a few bad feelings."

"I can see where it might."

"Enough about me and my charmed life. Tell me about you, or let me guess. A supermodel. Live in New York City. No dogs. One very demanding cat. Fight off the constant stream of wealthy, handsome admirers with the heels of your stilettos. Your admirers, not the cat's."

"Close. I live in Houston. Alone. No cats. No dogs. Not even a goldfish. No admirers. And this is my only pair of stilettos. They cost a small fortune, so I wouldn't dare risk breaking the heel in a fight. Basically, I'm your average dud."

"I'm not buying that. I see you more as a woman of mystery who possesses a multitude of intriguing secrets."

"No secrets. No mystery. The truth is my life is in a bit of chaos at the minute and I've escaped to Winding Creek for the weekend to put my concerns completely out of my mind."

"It's not some man who's caused the problem, is it? If it is, I can beat him up for you. Ooh-rah, and all that."

"There are no men in my life at present, at least none whose boots I'd let rest beneath my bed. What about you?"

"I fall in love every week or two."

"Really?"

"No. Got engaged once. She jilted me while I was in Afghanistan dodging IEDs."

"What a traitor. Want me to beat her up?"

"Would you?"

"Not in this dress. Bloodstains are too hard to remove."

He leaned back and stretched his legs in front of him. The denim of his jeans rubbed against her bare legs. Her breath caught.

Usually that was a warning sign of an all-too-frequent panic attack. But it wasn't anxiety that caused the tingly sensation deep inside her tonight.

She was so not ready for this with Luke or any other man. "I should probably go and see if I can help in the kitchen," she said.

"Why do I get the feeling you're trying to get rid of me?"

"You're welcome in the kitchen."

"Thanks, but I guess I'll go out back with the guys and trade in my empty beer bottle for a full one."

"Good idea."

They both stood.

He tipped his hat. "Nice chatting with you, Rachel Maxwell. I still think there's a mystery that I need to get to the bottom of."

And that was it. He walked away while she was

fighting the effect he was having on her. She couldn't even guess what Dr. Lindquist would think about this.

RACHEL DIDN'T MAKE it to the kitchen. She ran into her sister in the hallway.

"Do you have a few minutes, Rachel?"

One look and she could tell this would not be good. She should have known things were going too well. "What's wrong?"

"I had the TV on while Tucker was grabbing a shower. I caught the beginning of the evening news. You were the lead story."

"What now, or dare I ask?" Rachel said.

"Tucker's getting dressed. Let's talk in your bedroom." She followed Rachel and closed the door behind them.

"Hit me with it," Rachel said, not bothering to hide her frustration.

"You did tell me that you officially resigned from Fitch, Fitch and Bauman, didn't you?"

"Yes. I can't imagine that made the news."

"You're right. There was no mention of resignation. The announcement was that you, Rachel Maxwell, are going to lead the firm's dream team representing Hayden Covey in his murder trial."

Rachel threw up her hands in total exasperation. "I can't believe this. It's beyond ludicrous."

"Supposedly this is straight from the mouth of Hayden's mother."

Rachel dropped to the bed. "Mrs. Covey may have given the information to the reporter, but this is all Eric Fitch's doing. He no doubt told Senator and Claire Covey that my past would influence the jury. He used me as a bargaining chip to get this case and he hasn't bothered to let Mrs. Covey know I'm no longer in his game plan."

"I don't see how letting the lie go public will help him."

"No, but he has a plan to either get me back or convince the Coveys that he can win Hayden's case without me. I guarantee you that. Now I'm wondering if he was lying about being such great friends with the senator. If he was, he shouldn't have needed me to seal the deal."

"It's all backfired on him now," Sydney said. "How did he think this would possibly work out to his advantage?"

"I don't know, but I'm about to find out." Rachel walked over to the table and picked up her cell phone.

"Do you want me to leave you alone?" Sydney asked.

"Unless you want to be here for the fireworks."

"I think I'll wait for the recap."

Sydney let herself out the door.

Before Rachel could make her call, the phone rang.

Eric Fitch. Obviously, he'd seen the same evening news as Sydney had.

"Hello, Mr. Fitch. I'm assuming you have a valid explanation for Mrs. Covey announcing that I'm defending her son."

"Don't try to turn this into some conspiracy, Rachel. You were upset yesterday. So was I, but I'm sure we can get past this. You're too valuable to the firm for us to lose you."

"That wasn't what you said yesterday."

"I'm saying it now, and my son spoke for me yesterday when he told you how much we value you. I'm sure we can work something out. It would be a terrible mistake for you to resign just as we were about to make you a junior partner."

She dropped back to the edge of the bed. This was not playing fair.

"Come in on Monday and we'll talk terms on your promotion."

"I'm out of town and don't plan to be back in Houston before Tuesday at the earliest."

"Then we'll plan to talk then. In the meantime, don't give any statements to the press."

"That's the only promise I'm making."

"Of course. We'll talk. In the meantime, let's keep the business dealings out of the press."

"Perhaps you should tell Claire Covey that."

"I'll handle that."

Rachel was certain he would, in a way that would ensure that Claire Covey didn't take her money and high-profile case to another firm.

She cut the conversation off and went to find Sydney to give her the lowdown.

If she went back, she'd be the youngest junior partner at the firm. Everything she'd worked so hard for was practically in her grasp.

And yet her heart had never felt so heavy.

Chapter Seven

The ribs and brisket had been delicious. So had the baked potatoes, the field peas, the green salad and Dani's fabulous red velvet cupcakes left over from the afternoon's baby shower.

The food had been devoured and the kitchen cleaned a couple of hours ago. Luke lingered with some of the others at the large dining room table, talking and laughing the way he'd always imagined normal families did.

Mostly he was captivated by Rachel, who seemed to be actively avoiding any interaction with him. Actually, she'd hardly talked to anyone since dinner. Sydney had tried several times to pull her sister into the conversation. Her attempts had elicited no more than a word or two.

Rachel seemed lost in a world of her own, most likely the chaotic one she'd mentioned earlier. She definitely hadn't gone to her happy place.

Esther and the two youngsters had taken their

leave to find a quieter spot for a game of *Sorry*. The guys were still going strong, though the events of the day were catching up with Luke.

"The bull had it in for me," Tucker said, talking with his hands as much as his mouth. "It was personal. I knew it. The bull knew it. Everybody around the chutes knew it. No way was he going to give me the eight seconds I needed to win one of the most gorgeous silver belt buckles I'd ever seen."

"And you need another belt buckle so badly," Riley quipped. "Just to let you know, I'm kind of siding with the bull this time. No one ever gives him a buckle."

"What happened?" Dani asked, ignoring the brothers' good-natured ribbing.

"Not a dadburn thing. The bull got his revenge the easy way, ignored me completely. I pulled every trick I knew, and that contrary beast acted like he was out on a Sunday stroll.

"I could have stayed on it for half an hour and barely worked up a sweat."

"I take it that's a bad thing," Rachel said, finally joining in the conversation.

"I ended up with a paltry sixty-three points when I needed to be in the high eighties to take home the buckle."

"That doesn't seem fair," Dani said. "You did your part. It was the bull who goofed off."

"It's the luck of the draw," Tucker explained. "All

random. You get the bull they give you, but you seldom get one that doesn't give you a decent fight. Rodeo bulls are raised to give the rider all he can handle."

"Still seems like you got ripped off," Dani said. "Can you make an official complaint?"

"Yes, and unlike the official complaints he makes to me, they take note," Sydney teased.

"Thankfully, I was allowed a second attempt on a different bull, since Torture II didn't give me a fighting chance."

"Torture II?" Riley laughed and slapped a hand on his knee. "I love it."

"You would."

"Then what happened?" Grace asked.

"I took home the silver buckle."

The men jokingly booed. The women clapped, even Rachel. Maybe he was reading too much into her mood. She might just be tired.

Grace stood, stretched and patted her stomach. "I hate to leave such good company, but I not only eat for two these days, I sleep for two, as well. Today was a perfect day and I can't thank you all enough for my shower, but I'm truly exhausted."

"I'll get Jaci," Pierce said, "though she'll complain that I'm messing up her fun."

"Why not just let her go home with us and spend

the night?" Dani asked. "That way Grace and baby can sleep in tomorrow."

"I like it," Grace said. "And Jaci will love it. Do you have something she can sleep in?"

"It will be a little large, but she can wear one of Constance's T-shirts."

"Are we still on for the Sunday morning family trail ride?" Sydney asked.

"Sure, as long as you and Tucker are up for it," Pierce said. "Weather is supposed to be perfect in the morning, midfifties and clear. Nice day to take the Canyon Trail. Besides, I have everything ready for a cowboy breakfast when we reach the top."

"And I have a little special addition from Dani's Delights," Dani said.

"If it's your cinnamon rolls, count me in," Sydney chimed in. "Those are worth losing a little sleep over. For that matter, anything from your bakery is worth getting up early for."

"We'll drop Jaci off at your house in the morning, Grace, so she can change into her riding clothes," Dani said. "Pierce can take over from there."

"Sounds like a plan," Pierce said. "Why don't you join us, Luke? I know you're probably busy checking out the ranch, but we head out just after sunrise and are usually back here before ten. That will leave the rest of the day for whatever you've got planned."

Luke considered the offer. He'd love the opportunity to go riding with Rachel. But on the off chance that he'd had said or done something to upset her and put her in her edgy mood, he wasn't sure he should accept.

"I think the operative word here is family," Luke said. "I've horned in on your dinner tonight. I don't want to wear out my welcome my second day back in Winding Creek."

"It's a trail ride. The more the merrier," Riley said.

"Everyone might not feel that way," Luke cautioned. He turned to Rachel and waited for her to meet his questioning gaze.

She did but hesitated before nodding. "Of course you should come. Sunrise over the canyon shouldn't be missed."

Not the most resounding invitation he'd ever received, but he'd take it. He was looking for a way in, not out.

"I'll be here," he said. "Shall I trailer over my own mount? Arrowhead Hills seems to be well stocked with quarter horses."

"No need to go to the trouble unless you want to. We've got you covered," Riley said, "with horse and saddle. You can ride Torture III. You get Tucker's belt buckle if you stay on till breakfast."

Luke joined in the laughter.

Grace and Pierce went to tell their daughter good-night before heading to Pierce's truck for the very short ride to their cabin.

"I think I'll call it a night, as well," Rachel said. "It's been a long day. I'll see you all in the morning."

"Do you need to borrow some boots for the ride?" Luke teased.

"No, these will be fine." Rachel uncrossed her legs, showing off a gorgeous calf, then added a smile that knocked him for a wallop yet again. Her power over him appeared to be headed toward the danger zone despite the total lack of effort on her part.

"If you're going to be spending a lot of time on a ranch, you need some cowgirl boots."

"I'll keep that in mind—if I ever make a ranch my home."

Luke stood. "I'm out of here, too. But I gotta say, dinner was awesome."

"I thought it was good myself," Pierce said. "Even if we don't measure up to Esther's cooking."

"No one does," Sydney said.

"But Esther can't shoot like you, my sexy FBI bride," Tucker said as he stooped to give his wife a peck on the lips.

Rachel stepped closer to Luke. "I still have your jacket. I'll get it for you and meet you at the door."

"Sounds like a plan."

Luke reached the door just as Pierce was driving away. He stepped over to the porch railing, leaning his backside against it while he waited for Rachel. He wondered if this moment they'd have alone was by design or just happenstance.

Rachel joined him a minute later. She'd slipped out of her heels and into a pair of fluffy blue slippers. She held out his jacket and he crossed the porch to take it.

"Congratulations, Luke Dawkins. You not only survived but you hung right in there with the boisterous Lawrence brothers when they were in rare form. I'm impressed."

"Me, too. Never thought I'd say this, but it feels good to be back in Winding Creek—at least for tonight." That was mostly due to Rachel and would still likely change when dear old Dad was released from rehab and back on the ranch.

Luke refused to let that bother him while standing this close to Rachel. Moonlight streaked her luxuriant curls. Only a touch of lipstick remained on her full, tantalizing lips.

"You were awfully quiet tonight," he said. "The effect of the chaos you mentioned earlier?"

"Yes, but I'm working on shedding it from my life."

"It might help to talk about it with someone who's not family."

A stupid comment. Unlike his, her family was great. Why would she need a virtual stranger to confide in?

She pushed loose locks of hair behind her right ear and looked upward as if counting the stars that seemed close enough to touch.

"How much do you know about me?" she asked.

"Is this a trick question?"

"Not completely."

He reached across and took her small hand in his, half expecting her to pull away. When she didn't, a crazy protective urge swept through him. Only what or whom did she need protection from?

"I know you're gorgeous and you smell like lilacs." He trailed his fingers up her arm until they tangled into the delectable curls that fell past her shoulders. "What else should I know about you, Rachel?"

"Nothing that you won't find out for yourself soon enough."

Her words sounded like a pronouncement of lurking doom. A sense of hopeless dread chilled him as she backed against the front door and rested one hand on the knob. "I should go in now. We'll be up at dawn tomorrow."

"Then I guess this is good-night."

He tried to walk away. He honestly tried, but she looked so tempting. So irresistible.

He slid a thumb beneath her chin and nudged until she met his gaze. When she didn't turn away, his lips touched hers, brushing them like a feather, little more than a suggestion of a kiss. Even that was enough to send him reeling.

Rachel slipped her arms around his neck and kissed him back. Not shy or reluctant, but a bold, hungry kiss that set him on fire. He swayed against her, drunk on the thrill of lips on his, their tongues tangling, their breaths mingling.

Seconds later, she pulled away and placed an open hand against his chest, gently pushing him away. He was crazy with wanting her and was certain she could feel the pounding of his heart.

"See you tomorrow," she whispered as she opened the door and slipped back inside the house.

Tomorrow couldn't come too soon.

DAWN WAS LIGHTENING the sky before Rachel gave up on the tossing and turning and any chance of sound sleep. Her life was spinning out of control at a dizzying pace.

Two days ago, she'd had a career. She'd known what she would be doing from day to day. Admittedly, she'd still been struggling to move past the torture Roy Sales had put her through, but she was making progress.

Two days ago, she wasn't making headlines, another major detriment to defending Hayden. The terrors she was trying so hard to escape would be front and center.

People would stare. People would ask questions. Gossip magazines would feed on her trauma again.

Two days ago she hadn't met Luke Dawkins. Her stomach hadn't fluttered at his incidental touch. There had been no heated zings of attraction when a rugged, hard-bodied stranger spoke her name or met her gaze.

A kiss hadn't rocked her with desire and left her aching for more. She put her fingertips to her lips, and a craving for his mouth on hers burned inside her.

This was absolutely crazy.

She kicked off the covers, crawled out of bed, padded to the window and opened the blinds. The crescent moon floated behind a gray cloud. The universe held steady, day following night, season following season, the earth remaining on its axis century after century.

She didn't expect that kind of order in her life, but neither could she continue to let the demonic Roy Sales pull the strings and control her reactions.

She had to fight to get what she wanted—once she decided what that was. She'd spend the next two or maybe three days here in Winding Creek trying to figure it all out. Then she'd drive back to Houston and face Eric Fitch Sr. straight on.

There were no decisions to make about Luke Dawkins. Once he learned of her past, he'd see her through different eyes. And he'd definitely learn about her past, since she was making news again. He'd pity her, and then he'd move on.

Who could blame him? Her emotional baggage was killing her.

RACHEL, SYDNEY AND DANI were sipping coffee from disposable cups and watching Jaci and Constance raced around the corral while the guys saddled the morning's mounts.

The first sun rays were chasing away the moon from what was now a cloudless sky. The air was brisk. The breeze was gentle. Exactly the kind of morning she'd have ordered for a trail ride.

Except that Luke had not shown.

This was just the eye-opener she needed to realize last night's kiss didn't mean anything. Nor should it. God knew she had more on her plate than she could handle. Luke had overwhelming problems of his own.

Nonetheless, she couldn't stop herself from turning every few seconds to look over her shoulder for his truck approaching the horse barn.

Pierce sauntered over and joined in the children's game of chase. He caught Jaci, swooping her into his arms and then balancing her atop his shoulders.

"Time to climb into the saddle," he said. "Dreamer's getting impatient."

Riley stepped out of the horse barn, leading another horse that was saddled and tossing its head as if eager to be ridden. "Beauty's ready, too, Constance. I think she's more excited about getting some exercise than you are."

"Jaci and Constance are amazing kids," Sydney said. "Precocious and outgoing and both so sweet. I may have to start thinking about starting a family myself one of these days."

That got Rachel's full attention. "That's the first time I've heard you say that."

"Don't go buying any diapers. I'm not ready yet," Sydney said. "I'm still having too much fun fighting crime, but one day."

"I would have said the same thing until Constance fell into my life," Dani said. "Now I can't imagine life without her."

"They sit in the saddle like experienced horsewomen," Rachel said.

"Pierce and Riley both take up a lot of time with them, teaching them the basics about horses, including how to treat the animals. I swear I think Constance would much rather spend her time with horses than her school friends."

Tucker led a chestnut and a sorrel mare out of the barn, also saddled, bridled and ready to go. "Time to ride, ladies. This is Moonbeam, Rachel," he said, giving the chestnut a nose rub.

"She's beautiful."

"She's gentle and responds well even to a slight tug on the reins. She'll give you a great ride."

"Just listen to my gorgeous bull-riding hubby," Sydney said. "The way he talks about the Double K horses, you'd think he spent his time with horses instead of mean bulls."

"I told you I'm a man of many talents," Tucker teased.

"And so modest."

"Shouldn't we wait for Luke?" Dani asked.

"I had a call from him a few minutes ago," Pierce said as he fit the riding helmet on his young daughter. "He was out riding the fence line at dawn and came across a break in the fence from a fallen mulberry branch. He's fixing it before the cows head for greener pastures that might not belong to him."

"He'll be sorry he missed the cinnamon rolls," Riley said.

"And riding with all these beautiful women," Tucker added.

"He must agree with you," Pierce said. "He's still going to try to make it, but he said if he wasn't here when we got ready to start out, we should leave without him."

Rachel felt a tinge of relief. At least he wasn't avoiding her intentionally after she'd kissed him so ravenously last night—unless the break in the fence was just an excuse. Either way, she wouldn't have to face his questioning, pitying eyes if he'd already heard about the kidnapping.

She walked over to get acquainted with Moonbeam. Her experience with horses was not as extensive as the rest of the riding party's, but she had ridden some in college. Half her friends' families either owned a ranch or knew someone who did. That was Texas.

She heard the hum of the truck's engine just as they started their procession. Her mood improved dramatically.

"You guys go ahead," Riley called from the rear of the line. "Luke and I will catch up with you."

Rachel was just getting comfortable in the saddle when Luke slowed his horse and fell in beside her.

She glanced his way, and her heart skipped a couple of beats. There should have been a law against any man being that heart-stoppingly sexy.

He tipped his gray Stetson. A few locks of his hair fell over his forehead. The jagged angles and planes of his face were made more rugged by the dark whiskers on his chin. His denim jacket was open, revealing a black T-shirt that emphasized his hard body.

She took a deep breath and waited for her pulse to return to normal. "Glad you could join us," she said.

"Pleasure is all mine."

"Did you get your fence fixed?"

"Patched. It needs more extensive work like everything else around Arrowhead Hills except the horse barn. Dad's quarter horses live like kings. The other outbuildings are practically caving in. But enough about my troubles."

He pointed to the left. "Check out that view."

She did. They'd been climbing steadily since they left the horse barn. Grassy hillsides stretched out behind them, the rambling ranch house no longer visible.

"It's magnificent," she said.

At that moment, a tall, antlered buck and two does stepped out from the tree line a few yards ahead of them. She pulled the reins, slowing Moonbeam to a full stop. The deer remained still, staring back at her until a fluffy-tailed rabbit scurried past them.

The buck turned and raced back into the woods with the does at his heels.

"I forgot about all the wildlife in this part of Texas and how peaceful it is on the open range," Luke said. "No traffic jams. Clean air. The smell of the earth."

"The rural lifestyle does have a lot to offer," she agreed. "I should get to the Double K a lot more often than I do, but there never seems to be enough time."

"Which is exactly why you should spend more time here," Luke said. "That and the fact that Esther has a way of making everyone feel so welcome."

"She definitely does that."

Pierce dropped back to join them. "Having a problem?"

"Nope," Luke said. "Just stopped a moment to soak in the atmosphere."

"The scenery keeps getting better until we reach the canyon view," Pierce said. "Then it's phenomenal. We'll stop for breakfast there. Esther is bringing the food and supplies in the truck."

"I'm sure I'll be famished by then," Luke said. "And full as a tick when we head back."

They started along the trail again. Luke and Pierce immediately got into a conversation about cattle feed, hay and barn repairs.

Rachel left them behind and caught up with Sydney.

"I noticed you and Luke were riding together for a while," Rachel's sister commented.

"Only for a few minutes."

"So, what do you think of him other than the fact that he'd blow the top off any hunk-o-meter?"

"I hadn't noticed that."

"Really? When did you lose your eyesight?"

"Just kidding," Rachel confessed. "He's sexy. I'll give him that. And interesting."

"Then his attention isn't making you nervous."

"No, though strange men usually do. I suspect it has something to do with being here with all of you."

"I think that it's a good sign you're moving on."

"I hope you're right. It's been four months."

But moving on to what? It was peaceful here, but the real world was waiting to ambush her at the next turn.

ESTHER WAS WAITING for them at a flat, grassy spot with a nice view of Creek Canyon while still far enough away from the edge that Constance and Jaci weren't in danger of tumbling down the rocky decline. Neither of them ever slowed down.

In the Big Bend area of Texas, Creek Canyon would be considered more gulch than canyon, but it was impressive for the Hill Country.

Luke was familiar with the canyon from before, only he'd seen it from the other side on land that belonged to one of his baseball teammates. It was a favorite spot for going snake hunting, an activity they'd somehow thought fun back in the day.

Rachel didn't wait for his assistance but dismounted on her own and walked the horse over to a scrubby cluster of Texas walnut trees. She handed the reins to Pierce, who was already securing his and Jaci's mounts to a low branch.

There was no water for the horses, but they'd stopped at two streams on the way up, where the horses had drunk their fill.

The tailgate of Esther's four-wheel-drive pickup

truck was down, making a nice serving area for the thermoses of coffee and hot chocolate that were waiting for them. Within minutes everyone had a steaming mug in hand or at least within easy reach.

The women started unpacking and arranging the food from two huge picnic baskets. Luke went with Riley to gather wood for a stone fire pit that had clearly seen its share of use.

Once they had the fire going, Pierce filled a black cast-iron skillet with a spicy egg and chorizo mixture, and the marvelous odors filled the air. If Luke hadn't already been starving, the smells alone would have had him drooling.

Nothing like cooking real food in the outdoors. It beat those tasteless MREs he'd choked down in the Afghanistan wilderness by a county mile.

Everything seemed under control, so he stepped back from the fire and checked out the scenery. His gaze got no further than Rachel. She might be a city girl at heart, but she looked completely at home in this setting.

She was natural beauty. If she had on any makeup at all, he couldn't tell, and yet she was stunning.

"My sister-in-law is always an attention grabber," Tucker said, startling him.

Luke had been so lost in his appreciation of Rachel's beauty, he hadn't seen or heard Tucker approach from behind. No use to deny he'd been ogling. "She is striking."

"My wife thinks there's some chemistry firing between you and Rachel."

"I can't speak for Rachel, but I admit I find her fascinating. Is that a problem?"

"It could be."

"She's not married, is she?"

"No, and ordinarily I'd be the first to say she's tough enough to take care of herself. But she's had a traumatic few months—none of it her doing. I just wouldn't want to see her get hurt. That's all."

"I barely know her. I'm not planning to push myself on her, so you can relax if that's what you're worried about. Did Sydney ask you to talk to me?"

"No way. She thinks you and Rachel might be good for each other. I just figured it wouldn't hurt to mention that she's awfully vulnerable."

"I appreciate that. Is there more I should know?"

"Probably, but I'll leave that to Rachel. If I were you, I wouldn't push for more than she wants to say."

"I won't. Thanks for the update."

There it was again, innuendos that seemed to slide around straight facts. Luke usually liked a good mystery, but not this time. Mainly because he sensed it was troubling Rachel.

Tucker went back to the fire to relieve Pierce and

take over the job of warming the tortillas in a black iron skillet.

Rachel was helping Esther set out plates of sliced avocados, jalapeños and pico de gallo. Luke started to walk over and join them, but quickly reconsidered as a new idea came to mind.

He walked away from the group, pulled his phone from his pocket and did a Google search on Rachel Maxwell. Her image quickly stared back at him as well as a full page of offerings.

He started reading, his rage building with each sentence.

Rachel Maxwell had every reason to be vulnerable. She'd been through hell.

Chapter Eight

Roy Sales was walking by the TV in the community room when he heard the announcer say his name. He stopped and stared at his picture on the screen.

"Rachel Maxwell, one of the victims of the Lone Star Snatcher, will defend Hayden Covey against murder charges."

Damn. Had he heard that right?

"Shut up," Roy yelled at the old man who sat a few feet from him, chanting gibberish so loud Roy could barely hear what the pretty blonde TV announcer was saying.

Rachel's picture flashed on the screen. That was her, all right. She looked exactly as she had that first day he saw her—before he'd beaten the hell out of her and left her so bruised and bloody he could barely recognize her.

He strained to hear what the reporter was saying. The smart-mouthed attendants controlled the volume on the TV the way they controlled everything else in this stinking place.

He caught enough of the morning report to get the gist of the breaking news. His blood boiled. How dare she defend that rich son of a bitch after the way she'd talked about *him* after his arrest?

Rachel's words bellowed inside his head. *"Mentally unhinged." "A monster." "Crazy." "Psychopath."*

She was the reason he was locked up in this loony bin. But he had news for her. This wasn't over. He was smarter than every doctor in this horrible place.

He didn't swallow those mind-numbing pills they gave him every morning. He only played the game.

He'd be out of here soon. He had a plan. And then he'd get to finally watch Rachel Maxwell die.

Slow. Tortured. Begging for mercy as she gasped for her last breaths. He'd be every bit as evil as the monster she'd made him out to be.

"You just watch, Mommy. You'll be so proud of me."

Chapter Nine

As much as Rachel had enjoyed the first half of the trail ride, she was glad to get back to the horse barn. She had recognized the change in Luke even before they left the canyon.

He had come and sat down beside her while she finished her taco, but the conversation was strained. More telling was the fact that he didn't ride near her on the way back down the trail.

She'd seen him looking at something on his phone. Possibly another breaking news item. She and Hayden would take over the news cycle for a few days.

If they'd mentioned her, they would have talked about her abduction by Roy Sales. It was her horrifying claim to fame.

Before Rachel could dismount, Luke showed up and offered a hand to help her. "Ready to cool your saddle?"

"If that means am I ready to dismount, the answer is yes."

"That's what it means. Need some help?"

"No, thanks. I've got it."

Still holding the reins, she took hold of the saddle horn and threw her right foot back over the saddle. Moonbeam knew the procedure well, standing still until both of Rachel's feet were on solid ground.

She stretched, brushed off her tired bottom and then ran her fingers through Moonbeam's long, thick mane.

"How was your ride?" Luke asked.

"Enjoyable. What about you?"

"Great, and just what I needed to get me back in the fun part of the cowboy groove. So glad you and the rest of your crew invited me to intrude on your family fun."

He was trying to keep things light. Rachel would give him that, but she still sensed a difference in him.

He reached for the reins. "I'll take care of Moonbeam for you and see that she's put away properly."

"Thanks."

She started to walk away. Luke reached for her wrist with his left hand and held her back. "Any way we can talk privately after the horses are taken care of?"

She shrugged. "That's not necessary."

"I didn't mean to suggest that it was, but if you'd rather not, I understand."

Because he felt the need to say something about

what he'd learned, yet had to protect her tender feelings. Perhaps the worst was that there was some truth to the way her emotions could crater without warning.

"How did you find out?" she asked.

"I looked you up on the internet," he said, obviously knowing what she was referring to. "It's not exactly a secret."

"I know. I'm infamous. If you'd been in the country, especially in Texas, you'd already know all the gory details."

"I don't need the gory details. I just have one question."

"That's a shocker. Most people have a hundred."

"Where is Roy Sales now? Please tell me he's in prison."

"No. It's been just over four months, but unfortunately, he hasn't been deemed mentally competent to stand trial yet. He's being cared for in a maximum-security forensic mental hospital between here and Houston. It's supposedly state-of-the-art in treatment options."

"Probably a good place for him. Look, I know you're here to visit with your family this weekend, but it would be great if you had some time to fit me into your schedule."

"I smell like horseflesh."

"Nothing wrong with that. But it doesn't have to

be now and I promise this has zero to do with the kidnapping, if that's what you're concerned about."

"Then what is it you want to talk about?"

"Us."

"There is no us, Luke. We just met. I live in Houston. You have a father with health concerns to take care of in Winding Creek."

"Correct me if I'm wrong, but I kind of got the idea we have a little attraction going here."

"The kiss. I can explain that. Well, actually, I can't, but we shouldn't try to make more of that than it was. I think I got carried away in the moment."

"Why not check it out and see where it goes? I'm not necessarily talking sex. Talk is good. A beer or two. A long walk. Dinner in town or dancing at the roadhouse. I guess that's still going strong."

He made this sound so natural, but nothing in her life had been natural since Sales had held her in captivity. Seeing where this could go might be dangerous. She should just send him away.

Yet she couldn't deny how desperately she wanted to see him again.

"I'd invite you to Arrowhead Hills for lunch," Luke said, "but I think the whole house needs to be fumigated or at the very least scrubbed with bleach and a generous application of elbow grease. I don't know if my dad's eyesight is failing and he can't see the built-up crud and mildew or if he's so used to it he doesn't notice or possibly care."

"Scrubbing away crud and grime. Cleansing. Physical activity that requires no brain cells. Call me crazy," Rachel said, "but I find that extremely alluring today."

"I wouldn't think a highfalutin attorney like you ever stooped to such mundane tasks."

"I'll have you know there is nothing highfalutin about me, though it has been many a moon since I've gotten on my hands and knees to scrub a floor."

"Sounds intriguing," he teased. "Forget the cleaning, but I am serious about wanting to spend some time with you this afternoon."

"I can't make any promises until I see what Sydney has planned. I get to see my sister so seldom, but I still have to share her with her bull-rider hubby. I can give you a call later."

"Whenever you can get away is fine. Just give me enough warning to grab a shower. I'll likely be checking out the livestock. Dad's record keeping is like deciphering a secret code."

"Ugh. Does Esther have your phone number?"

"Yes, and so does Pierce. He's going to give me a cram course on modern ranching one afternoon this week. I'd write the number down for you, but I don't have a pen on me."

Moonbeam tossed her head and pawed the dirt.

"That's horse talk for 'I've had enough of this,'" Luke said. He tipped his hat and grinned. "I'll be waiting for your call."

Amazing how he could start her heart spinning with just a smile.

He thought her talk of scrubbing was facetious, but something physically demanding might be exactly what she needed. At least she'd be doing something useful.

But she had to admit that getting rid of grease and grime would be the weirdest first date ever.

Except this wouldn't be a date. They couldn't take this too far, but it was possible they could be friends.

SYDNEY HAD STOPPED to wait on Rachel about halfway down the worn path from the horse barn to the big house. Rachel hurried to catch up.

"You look flushed," Sydney said.

"Too much wind and sun."

"Nice try. I think it's the Luke Dawkins effect."

"I have no idea what you're talking about."

"You know exactly what I'm talking about. The way you two look at each other could ignite a five-alarm fire."

"We're practically strangers."

"That has nothing to do with chemistry."

"There is no place in my life for chemistry."

Sydney linked her arm with Rachel's. "Maybe, but

there's nothing wrong with enjoying the company of a hunk like Luke who also happens to be a nice man."

"How do you know that?"

"He's a former marine, with a couple of medals for bravery, according to Esther. He's giving up his life temporarily to take care of an unhealthy father who basically disowned him when he was just a teenager. Esther likes him and she's a great judge of character."

"You have this all figured out, Sydney, which means you're spending too much time worrying about me."

"Not worried. Encouraging. Just because you spend time with a man doesn't mean you have to hop in bed with him—although I'm not knocking that, either. But I'll leave it up to you to know when the time is right."

"Thank you for that vote of confidence." Not that she was sure she was worthy. "You know, you and Dr. Lindquist think alike on so many things. You would have made a great psychologist."

"Or perhaps he should have become an FBI agent. I wish your psych was here right now."

"To encourage me to jump Luke's bones?"

"No." Her tone became strained. "But he'd do a better job of sharing more bad news than I will."

Rachel's spirits plunged. "What now?"

"It's nothing horrible—or urgent. It's—"

"Don't bother sugarcoating it," Rachel interrupted.

"Okay. I got a call last Wednesday from Dr. Leonard Kincaid."

Rachel's stomach knotted. "What's wrong with your health?"

"Nothing. Dr. Kincaid is Roy Sales's psychiatrist."

A shudder ripped thought Rachel. "They didn't release him. Please tell me they didn't say he was unfit to stand trial and just set him free."

"No. He's still in the maximum-security facility. You're safe. That I'm sure of, one of the perks you get from having a sister with the FBI."

"Then why would Sales's doctor call you?"

"He was trying to get in touch with you, but since you changed your cell phone to a secure number to avoid the constant harassment of the media, he couldn't reach you."

"And I want to keep it that way. Apparently you didn't give Dr. Kincaid my number."

"No, but I told him I'd give you a message."

"Which is?"

"All he would say is that it's important he talk to you. He wouldn't give me any of the pertinent reasons why. He claimed doctor/patient privilege."

"You're an FBI agent. I thought you were cleared for everything, even doctor/patient privilege."

"It doesn't work quite that way. Anyway, he wanted me to tell you that he'd very much like to talk to you, preferably in person."

"In person, like in my going to the facility where Roy Sales is being treated? That's not going to happen."

"He said he'll travel to you."

"That makes zero sense. Everything I could tell him about Sales is well documented."

Rachel stopped walking as they approached the house. "I know you've had time to think about this and I trust your judgment. Can you think of any good reason I should get involved with Sales or his psychiatrist?"

"There is one positive side to at least talking to him."

"Which is?"

"The sooner Roy Sales faces trial, the sooner you can put all this totally behind you. If you have any insight—even information you don't think is important that could make that happen faster—it might be worth talking to Kincaid."

"Then you think I should call him?"

"It's not my decision, Rachel. I only want what's best for you, but if you do agree to seeing him, I'd like to be with you."

"As a sister or as an FBI agent?"

"Both, but mostly as a sister who doesn't want to see Roy Sales put you though any more torment."

"This just seems so bizarre," Rachel said. "Did the

doctor say if he's talked to the other kidnapping victims?"

"I asked. He said he hadn't and didn't judge it to be useful at this point."

Rachel kicked at a small stone that was in her path and sent it flying toward Esther's front porch. "So this is personal between Roy Sales and me? Something Kincaid thinks I know that the other victims don't?"

"I got that impression, but it could be that he thinks your experience as a criminal defense attorney might make you a more valuable source of information."

"That's possible, I guess."

"You don't have to decide this minute, especially with all that's going on with your career. Take your time. Think about it. And remember, you can always tell him no. You aren't required to help Roy Sales in any way."

"The only help I'd give is to make certain he's never free to torture and murder again."

"That's what we all want."

"I'll think about calling Dr. Kincaid, but right now I'm not leaning that way. If he called you on Wednesday, why are you just now mentioning it to me?"

"I wanted to tell you in person, but then you were dealing with the job situation and I didn't want to lay more problems on you the minute I saw you."

"Which granted me a short reprieve," Rachel said.

"A day or two to adjust to one problem before the next punches me in the gut. That's about average."

"You don't have to deal with this now or ever."

But she'd be thinking about it, and just hearing Sales's name cast a shadow over her world.

She had a nauseating suspicion that Roy Sales was orchestrating all this, trying to pull her back into his sphere of evil for his own sick pleasure.

His madness was real, but that didn't mean he wasn't smart enough to manipulate a whole team of psychiatrists.

Too bad she couldn't just scrub every memory of him from her life. But there was no cleanser that strong in all the world.

BY TWO IN the afternoon, life at the Double K Ranch had settled into a quiet, sleepy Sunday afternoon bliss. Esther was stretched out on the couch watching a Lifetime movie. Sydney and Tucker were taking advantage of the unseasonably warm weather to attend a winter festival in a neighboring town.

They'd invited Rachel to go with them, but she had enough sense to know it was private time together they were looking for. With their careers taking them in different directions, they cherished the time they had together.

Sydney truly loved working with the FBI. She thrived on the excitement and even the danger, the same way Tucker couldn't imagine life without the rodeo.

Indications were the lifestyle worked for them. Rachel envied them that.

She'd thought she'd found her niche in life, and now she wasn't even sure she wanted to take the firm's very generous promotion offer. Her priorities seemed to be shifting by the hour.

She was tempted to call Luke Dawkins, but what was the point? Roy Sales wasn't physically strangling her the way he did in her recurring nightmares, but he was emotionally strangling her.

Luke was interested in getting to know her better, and that would lead to the attraction building. How could she trust herself in a romantic entanglement with her life in a tailspin? She had nothing to offer but trouble. She liked him too much to add her burdens to his.

Weakening in her resolve not to call him, she walked back to the guest bedroom and grabbed her purse and her keys. She didn't bother to change from the denim cutoffs and loose-fitting T-shirt she'd changed into after lunch. She had to get out of here.

Her phone rang as she was pulling into a parking spot on Main Street. She answered as she climbed out of the car and started walking. "Hello."

"Hi, Rachel. Glad I caught you."

"Luke." Her pulse quickened at the sound of his

voice. This was quickly swelling out of hand. "I'm sorry I didn't call."

"Me, too. That's why I called you. How about I pick you up and we take a drive, give me the opportunity to see how the area's changed since I moved away?"

"What happened to our scrubbing hoedown?"

"Believe me, this mess is more than you want to tackle. I don't even know where to begin."

"In the kitchen, of course. Kitchens always have more grease and grime than any other area."

"You're serious, aren't you?"

"I am. My brain is exhausted, but my muscles are atrophying."

"In that case, I'll pick you up as soon as I make a run to the store for some supplies."

"I'm already in town. I'll stop off at the market, pick up the supplies and drive to your place. And don't worry, I won't charge you the full price for my billable hours."

"I should have known there was a catch."

"Well, you are dealing with an attorney."

He gave her easy-to-follow directions. She turned to start back to the car, but then stopped and looked around her. Two youngsters holding doubled-dipped cones of chocolate ice cream walked past her, the melted treat dripping from their mouths and hands.

Their youthful parents followed close behind, laughing and chatting and holding hands like lovers.

Small-town Texas. Friendly. Safe.

Until that facade had been shattered by a psychopath who'd chosen his victims from this very street. Familiar fear crawled inside her like a hairy spider. She stopped walking and looked around as the apprehension swelled.

No place was ever completely safe.

She walked a few feet and then stopped to stare into the Christmas shop. Even in January, miniature villages, their roofs topped with fake snow, filled the display windows. A little girl walked up and stopped next to her, her nose pressed against the glass, no doubt already dreaming of Christmas.

Rachel took deep breaths until the unwanted flare of tenseness eased. Then she quickly walked to her car and drove the short distance to the market.

She stocked up on cleansers, protective gloves and some fruit, chips and salsa in case she needed some calorie fortification for the tasks at hand. Having no idea what kind of munchie Luke liked, she picked up some peanuts and a couple of packs of cheese crackers and cookies.

The last stop on the way to checkout was the beer aisle. She figured she couldn't go wrong with that.

Once she checked out, she made a phone call to Sydney to let her know she would be spending the afternoon with Luke Dawkins. There was no answer. She left a message.

Minutes later, she was on her way to Arrowhead Hills.

Still a bit uneasy, she tried to soothe her mind. How much trouble could she possibly get into scrubbing floors with Luke Dawkins?

Chapter Ten

Luke stuck his head into the oven for one last check. "Spotless as new and ready for inspection," he announced. "My guess is for the first time in years. I could almost swear there was part of a pizza I warmed up eleven years ago still stuck to the top shelf."

"Gross." Rachel walked over and checked it out. "I'm impressed. I'd actually eat something cooked in there now."

"And mess up my clean oven? No way," he protested. "We're not turning on that oven for anything."

"Not even for pizza?"

"There might be some exceptions."

He leaned his backside against the counter—which was also spotless—and watched Rachel as she went back to returning foods to the dust- and crumb-free pantry.

"Now that we've thrown away everything that was out-of-date, you'll have to restock," she said.

"Yes, ma'am. Another day. It's gotta be Miller time by now."

"Don't tell me a little housework is harder than being in the marines."

"Only difference is you're holding me hostage with a broom instead of enemy fire."

She returned the last item to the top shelf of the pantry and surveyed the finished product.

Luke walked behind her and put his arms around her waist. "Do you have any idea how sexy you look right now?"

"I suppose you're about to tell me you're turned on by the fragrance of bleach."

"Is that what that is?" He sniffed behind her ear. "I thought it was awfully pungent for perfume."

He was telling the truth about her being sexy and so damn easy to be around. But she was right about one thing. Now that he knew, he couldn't help thinking about what that monster had put her through.

He'd love to meet that guy in a dark alley with only their fists between them. Fat chance he'd get that opportunity, but it riled him to think the guy wasn't tried and sentenced to life in prison. There was no doubt the guy was evil, but he wondered just how crazy he really was.

Rachel was vulnerable like Tucker had warned him. She'd have to be after what she'd been through. But she was also tough and smart. And energetic.

"Wonder Woman in denim," he said.

She straightened a can of peas and then closed the panty door. "Are you summoning a superpower to rescue you from the slave driver attorney?"

"I was talking about you. You are amazing. Up at sunrise to go horseback riding. Sun's setting and you're still going, gung ho, unlike the poor cowboy trying to keep up with you." He nibbled her ear.

She stepped out of his arms. "This isn't work. It's therapy, and you can't let your father return to this. When will he be coming home?"

"I don't know. I have an appointment with his doctor tomorrow. I'll stop by and see Dad after that. After the greeting he gave me yesterday, I'm not sure he wants to come home if I'm here."

"It can't be that bad."

"Wait till you meet him. Which is a great idea now that I think about it. Why don't you ride into town with me tomorrow? One look at you and he'll forget I'm even around."

"How old is he?"

"Sixty-nine, but he's not dead. He'll notice you."

Luke opened the refrigerator and took out two cold beers. He opened them both and handed one to her.

She sipped and then turned slowly, pointing out their day's accomplishments as she did. "Appliances shiny clean. Countertops and sink sparkling and hygienic. Cabinets organized. Kitchen window washed, ceiling fan blades dusted. Woodwork and floors thoroughly scrubbed."

"I couldn't have done it without you. Actually, I probably wouldn't have attempted it without you. How about we take our beers and go sit outside?" Luke suggested. "My muscles ache. I think I'm allergic to all this cleanness."

"You'll forget that once you get my bill."

"Now you're scaring me—unless, of course, you want to work it out in trade."

"I'm not even going there."

RACHEL WAS TIRED to the bone, but even that didn't prevent her from reacting to every look and touch from Luke. She'd practically gone into orbit when he nibbled her ear.

Working barefoot and shirtless, his jeans riding a few inches below his waist and his muscles flexing, had further certified his hunk status.

That was just the start of what excited her about him. There was no pretense with him. Great sense of humor. Virile and masculine to the core but without any of the machismo that would have made her uncomfortable.

Still she felt guarded, afraid that if she ever let her full fears seep out, they'd explode and spill all over her like a deadly poison.

Luke was beside her, his hand on the small of

her back, protective and possessive, as they walked through the house and onto the porch. The sun was low in the sky, but the humidity and temperature still made it feel like a summer day. The cold beer felt good in her hand. She suspected a cool shower would feel even better after all the work they'd put in this afternoon.

She brushed a few wisps of hair from her face, pushed them behind her ears and headed for the old porch rocker.

She started to sit down and then squealed and jumped backward as a large scorpion dropped from the arm of the chair and fell onto the seat.

Luke flew into action, knocking the scorpion out of the chair. The despicable arachnid fell onto the porch and took off in her direction, its stinger curved and ready to strike.

She dashed for the edge of the porch and climbed onto the railing, holding her feet in the air and almost toppling over the back, butt first.

"Kill it," she screamed. "Don't let it get away."

Thinking quickly, he didn't stamp it with his bare feet but grabbed a heavy pot of dead flowers and crashed it on top of the scorpion. The pot broke into a thousand pieces.

The scorpion wiggled like a creature from *The Walking Dead* before finally lying unmoving in the grave of sunbaked dirt and pottery shrapnel.

Luke broke into laughter.

"There is nothing funny about scorpions," she scolded.

"No, but can I see that rail-riding stunt again? You may be ready for bronc riding."

She planted her feet back on the porch. "Very funny. And here I was about to claim you as my hero."

"In that case, scorpions are nothing. Wait until you see my finesse with a rattlesnake."

"No demonstration needed. I'll take your word on that."

She walked to the busted pot, stooped and started picking up the larger pieces of broken pottery. She kept a wary lookout for any other bug that might be hiding in the chunks of dried earth.

"Just pile the pieces on the step," Luke said after the two of them had gathered the larger pieces. "I'll get a trash bag."

She did and then she spotted a hose that was hooked up to a faucet on the side of the porch. Exactly what she needed to wash the dirt off the porch before it got tracked back inside and ended up on her freshly scrubbed kitchen floor.

She turned on the hose and adjusted the nozzle to a jet spray. The powerful flow made quick work of getting rid of the dirt and tiny pieces of pottery.

Now that she was at it, she decided to wash off the rest of the porch and the old rocking chair that might have any number of creepy, crawly things hiding beneath the weathered slats.

She didn't hear or see the front door open and wasn't aware Luke had rejoined her as she turned to aim the spray at the chairs.

He yelped.

She turned to see him wiping water from his face and eyes with both hands. His hair was dripping wet. So were his jeans.

She aimed the spray into the yard. "Oops. Sorry."

"Oops?" Luke yelled. "Too late for 'oops' and 'sorry.' That was an act of war." He started toward her.

She backed up, sprayed him again and then dropped the hose and ran. He picked up the hose and aimed the spray at her. In minutes, they were both soaking wet.

By the time Luke dropped the hose, he was laughing hysterically. She started laughing, too. Hard. Uncontrollable. She laughed so hard that tears started running down her face.

Laughed the way she hadn't laughed in months and maybe longer.

Then, as if someone had slapped her across the face, the tears became bitter and the laughter became choking sobs. Tremors shook her body.

Luke ran to her, alarm firing in his eyes. "What's wrong? Are you hurt? Or angry?"

"No," she murmured through the painful sobs. "I don't know what's wrong with me. I don't know why I'm crying."

She expected him to back away fast from the crazy woman having a meltdown over too much fun. Instead he picked her up and cradled her in his arms as he carried her inside the house. "Cry if you need to, baby. Cry all you want. I'm here for you and I'm not going anywhere."

He settled in on the brown leather sofa, still holding her in his strong arms.

"I never used to lose it like this," she whispered through the sobs and the knot in her throat. "I'm sorry. I'm so sorry."

"You've done nothing to apologize for, Rachel. Your emotions are raw and have every reason to be, but maybe it's time you stop trying to be so strong. Maybe it's time you stop holding all the hurt and fears inside and just let them pour out."

"I think maybe it is," she admitted. More important, for the first time since the abduction, she thought maybe she could.

Chapter Eleven

"I can't remember the last time I ate canned chicken noodle soup," Rachel said.

Luke wiped his mouth with a paper napkin. "Me, either. It's better than I remember or else the mess hall food set a really low bar for tasty."

"Good that it's edible, since it's basically the only food option available now that the expired choices have been eliminated."

"Yeah. I guess I should buy some staples, like you said. I can't expect Esther and the Lawrence brothers to feed me all the time, though it's worked well so far."

"Wait until you try Esther's award-winning peach cobbler and homemade ice cream. If you can keep from going back for seconds, you have no taste buds."

Rachel tugged a bit on the soft cotton blanket she was wearing sarong-style, conscious every second that she was naked beneath it.

She'd been trembling when Luke carried her inside, chilly after the bout with the hose, but mostly emotionally shaken.

He'd insisted she get out of her wet clothes. He'd given her the blanket and pointed her to the bathroom. While she'd showered under a refreshing spray, he'd thrown her jeans, shirt and undies in the wash.

Her hair was still wet when she'd met him back in the kitchen, once again wrapped in her cotton blanket. A box of tissue rested on the corner of the table. Obviously, Luke was prepared for the next meltdown.

He'd changed out of his wet jeans and was wearing clean ones and a sky blue pullover. But still no shoes. Inexplicably, his bare feet made the scene cozier, made him seem more familiar, like a friend she'd known for years instead of a stranger she was considering spilling her guts to.

She spooned up another mouthful of warm soup, but this time it didn't soothe. As she swallowed, the sickening image of Roy Sales stamped itself into her brain.

"We can talk whenever you're ready," Luke said, likely fearing from her facial expression that she was on the verge of another flood of tears.

"Not that I'm pressing," Luke added, "but if you keep things bottled up inside you too long, they have a way of eating you alive."

"I've found that out the hard way," she admitted. "I don't know where to start."

"How about the beginning?"

"You do have a way of cutting to the chase, Luke Dawkins."

"I'm a simple man."

That, she wasn't buying, but she trusted him and that was what mattered now. "I left my house on Friday, the eighth of September. We'd just won a difficult case that should have ended days before. I'd already booked a spa resort in Austin for some much-needed R and R."

"Were you traveling alone?"

"Yes. I often do, or at least I did. I haven't traveled anywhere except here to see Sydney since then. I spent that Friday night in the small town of La Grange and then, on the recommendation of the owner of the B and B, I drove to the quaint western town of Winding Creek on Saturday morning."

"Was that your first time in Winding Creek?"

"Yes, at that point neither Sydney nor I had ever met Esther Kavanaugh or the Lawrence brothers. I stopped at Dani's Delight for coffee and a pastry, so luckily I met Dani that day. As it turned out, she was an important lead to Sydney's finding me."

"Thank goodness you stopped in for coffee."

"Right. When I left the bakery, there were still several more hours of daylight, so I took the meandering scenic drive back to the interstate."

The interstate she'd never reached.

"A few miles out of town, a cowboy pulled up beside me in his pickup truck and started motioning and hollering at me to pull over."

"Was he alone?"

"Yes. I lowered my window but couldn't understand what he was saying. I considered pulling over, but something about the situation made me uncomfortable, especially since my car was running fine."

"Were there other cars around?"

"No. I'd passed other cars since leaving Winding Creek, but there were no vehicles in sight then. No houses. Nothing but barbwire, pastures and cattle."

The pressure began to build inside her. Tears burned at the back of her eyes. She gritted her teeth and kept talking.

"I decided to keep driving until I reached the highway and a service station where I could safely check things out. I slammed my foot down on the accelerator and drove as fast as I dared on the curving road."

"But he kept coming?"

"Stayed right on my tail. I was afraid he was going to try to force me off the road. Then I heard what sounded like an explosion. I checked the rearview mirror and saw sparks and smoke."

"Gunshots?"

"No." Her voice was barely a whisper. Her insides quivered. She forced the words to keep coming. It was the first time since she'd given the police the information that she'd retold the events in such detail.

"I assumed my gas tank had exploded. I panicked, pulled to the shoulder and jumped from the car."

"Which is exactly what the low-life son of a bitch was counting on."

"Yes. It was the same strategy he'd used with the others, though no one knew that at the time. When I looked up, Sales was running toward me.

"I felt his fists hammer my face. That was the last thing I remembered until I woke up in a dark, dank room with my eyes swollen almost closed and my body covered in bruises."

Luke muttered a few curses. "Sorry, but it's too damn bad you weren't carrying a .45. That's the only straight talking a bastard like that understands."

"I wouldn't have known how to use it."

"It's time you learn, though hopefully you'll never encounter a psychopath like Sales again. I'm sorry for interrupting you," Luke said. "Go on. I'll keep quiet, but I am serious about your learning to shoot."

"The rest is a nightmare," she said. "Are you sure you want to hear it?"

"I'm sure *I* can handle it. You're the one being faced with the horrors again. How are you holding up?"

"I'm good." Not true, but she'd gotten this far. There was no reason not to get it all out now.

"When I came to, I was lying on a thin pallet on a hard floor. I was in such pain I could barely move and had no clue where I was, only that there was a good chance the monster who'd attacked me was nearby.

"The room was windowless and the only light came from a strip of illumination creeping in from beneath a closed door. I was sure the door would be locked, but I had to try it, so I scooted stomach-down across the floor.

"All for nothing. The door was locked. I was the monster's prisoner. I had never been so afraid in my life. I hope to never be again."

Luke stretched his arms across the table and reached for Rachel's hands. She pulled away, stood and started to pace the kitchen. She had to get through this on her own. Leaning on his strength would steal the courage she needed.

Her thoughts rambled, her fears mingling with her words as they spilled from her mouth without filter.

Sales's maniacal laughter. The cold, dead cruelty in his eyes. The periods of hunger and thirst and the knowledge that she'd lost all control. The unending fear and the paralysis that hit when she heard his footsteps outside the door.

The constant prayers that Sydney would find her before it was too late.

Rachel stopped pacing and stared out the window

into the darkness as the blistering mental scars burst into malignant abscesses all over again.

"I wasn't the only one held captive in that hell-hole," she said. "There were three others, though I never saw them until the night we were rescued.

"That was the night Roy realized his horrid abduction game was coming to an end. He set fire to the compound and attempted to burn all of us alive. I can't smell smoke or see a fire without reliving that night. I'm not sure I ever will."

She finally got up the nerve to face Luke again. His lips were a thin line, his face jagged angles, his jaw protruded.

"The Lone Star Snatcher." Luke spit the infamous title like a curse. "That's how the internet article referred to him."

"That's what the FBI termed him," Rachel explained. "I didn't know any of that until after my rescue. I just thought of him as the monster."

"More fitting, if there were a word to describe a devil in the body of a man."

"He is evil incarnate," Rachel said. "I'm sure he hasn't changed. How could he after the beastly crimes he's committed? He murdered a runaway teenage girl who'd been living on the streets of San Antonio. He killed Esther's husband, Charlie, in cold blood—in his own barn. She found him with a bullet through his head."

"Charlie? He murdered Charlie Kavanaugh? I didn't know."

"Only because you were halfway around the world in a news vacuum. That's another long story, another unthinkable crime Sales committed with no remorse. Sydney could better fill you in on that information."

Rachel squeezed her eyes tight to hold back the salty tears that were pushing for release. "Two weeks in captivity have torn me apart. Charlie Kavanagh is dead and Esther will suffer from that grief every day for as long as she lives."

Rachel buried her face in her hands as tears began to rain down her cheeks. Reliving the horror hadn't helped. How could she have believed it would?

She heard the scrape of Luke's chair and the slap of his bare feet on the kitchen floor as he walked over and stopped behind her. His hands clasped her shoulders and then pulled her around to face him.

"You are one of the bravest people I've ever met, Rachel, and believe me, that's saying a lot." He dabbed at her tears with a tissue.

"No. I'm not brave at all. I'm stuck in this nauseating time warp of nerves and fear. The horror of Roy Sales won't let go."

"It will. It just takes time." He reached for more tissues and put a wad of them to her nose. "Blow."

She did, then sniffled and tried to stop shaking.

Luke pulled her into his arms and she let her head rest on his broad shoulder. "I'm sorry," she murmured.

"Don't be. You can cry on my shoulder all night if that's what it takes to make you feel safe. I'll be here as long as you need me."

"Thanks, Lu—"

Her words were lost in the touch of his lips on hers. Her mind screamed this was the wrong time, the wrong place. Her body ignored the warnings.

She needed his touch, needed his strength. Needed him.

The kiss consumed her, taking her breath away. His fingers tangled in her hair as he pulled her closer.

She splayed her hands across his back, loving the feel of his bare flesh and the strong cords of his muscles.

He moaned her name.

Her insides became molten.

And then all on its own, the cotton loops worked free and the blanket dropped and pooled at her feet.

Chapter Twelve

Luke stared at Rachel, his body rock hard, his breath ragged.

Her arms fell to her sides. She didn't reach for the blanket but just stood there inches away from him. The same need that rocketed through him was mirrored in her beautiful, dusky eyes.

The urge to take her right here and now was savage. On the table, on the floor, against the wall. He ached to touch her perfect breasts, to suck the nipples that stood at attention like bullets.

He fisted his hands to keep from running them down the smooth flesh of her belly to find the sweet heat hidden beneath the triangle of dark hair.

He'd never wanted a woman more.

Yet his brain was yelling no. She'd just bared her soul to him. She was vulnerable. Making love might be fantastic for him, but she might wake up tomorrow with deep regrets.

Somehow he found the strength to look away. He

stooped, picked up the blanket and wrapped her in it again. "Why does this feel like I'm rewrapping the best gift I've ever received?"

"Why are you?" she asked.

The truth hit hard. It was because he didn't want to be the guy who'd just happened to be there when she faced all her fears and weaknesses head-on. He didn't want to be a one-night stand remembered with remorse. Not with Rachel.

Her phone rang, saving him from having to put feelings he didn't fully understand himself into words.

She walked over to the table and picked up her phone. "It's Sydney."

"Better take it," he said. "She's probably worried that you're still scrubbing floors."

She took the call and he reluctantly went to get her clothes from the dryer.

"Hi, Sydney."

"Hi, yourself, and where are you?"

"At Luke Dalton's place. I left you a message."

"Hours ago. Are you okay?"

"I'm great."

"Did you have dinner?"

"I did." Canned soup while wearing a blanket. That would take a lot more explaining than Rachel cared to share.

"At the risk of being the nosy younger sister, when are you coming home?"

"That's not nosy. I'll be leaving here within the next half hour."

"I'll see you then. Can't wait to hear about your afternoon."

"Now you're being nosy?"

"Sister's privilege."

They had always shared a lot with each other. This time Rachel would keep a few intimate details to herself. Like how wildly her heart had beat when she stood naked in front of Luke. Like how much she'd wanted him to claim her like some morally unencumbered Neanderthal.

Only he wasn't like that. He was a decent guy, a caring cowboy who'd turned away when she'd stood before him naked.

Luke returned as she finished the call and broke the connection. Her clean and dry clothes were draped over his arm.

"You'd best change into these," he said. "If that blanket were to fall again, I make no promises of controlling my urges or my sanity."

"It's getting a bit warm anyway," she said, "and I need to be going."

"I'll drive you home," he said.

"That's not necessary."

"It is," he assured her. "No cowboy worth his spurs

would let a beautiful woman drive herself home on these old ranch roads after dark."

"I'd only have to come back in the morning for my car."

"Not if you go with me to visit my dad in San Antonio. I'd pick you up whatever time you say."

"You don't need me for that."

"Probably not, but I'd really enjoy your company. I would like your feedback on what the doctor says about Dad's prognosis. And if the weather holds, we could follow the unpleasantness with a margarita and a stroll along the River Walk."

"Your invitation just gained a lot more appeal, Luke Dawkins."

"I can add more exciting options, if you're interested," he teased.

She started to take her clothes back to the bedroom to change but stopped at the door. "Just tell me one thing, Luke. Why didn't you make a move on me tonight when the sexual tension was going through the roof?"

"For the record, not touching you was one of the hardest things I've ever done in my life, and that includes combat. But I know how difficult it was for you to open up about Roy Sales. I didn't want to confuse the emotional lines between lover and confidant."

"So you were protecting me?"

"Yes, but that wasn't the whole of it. When we make love for the first time, and believe me, I'm counting on that happening, I want you to have nothing on your mind but me."

Any doubt of how hard she was falling for Luke vanished. "Then all you're asking for is perfection?"

"Damn straight."

"HAVE A SEAT and Dr. Riche will see you in a few minutes."

Luke and Rachel did as the nurse instructed. Rachel sat on the end of a deep blue sofa. He moved a health magazine out of the way and sat down next to her.

The drive from Winding Creek to the doctor's office had been slightly awkward, his attempts at casual conversation falling flat. The sensual sizzle from last night was still there but lurking beneath the surface in the bright light of day.

He still had no idea where he'd gotten the power to control his libido when that blanket hit the floor. It made him weak just thinking about it.

The attraction was out in the open now, but did he dare act on it? She was struggling with fears he couldn't fully understand. He suspected no one could unless they'd faced what she had.

The last thing he wanted to do was hurt her.

And there was Alfred, a father who needed but

clearly did not want Luke's help. A father who was a stranger by choice. A man who had always lived life on his terms and who'd suddenly lost the ability to function without assistance.

Even if everything was in their favor, Luke couldn't imagine a lasting relationship developing between Rachel and him. She was a high-powered attorney in Houston. He was an ex-marine still trying to find where he fit in life as a civilian.

"Are you sure you want me to go in to see the doctor with you?" she asked. "I can wait here if you'd like more privacy."

"You may as well hear the worst—or the best—from Dr. Riche. Otherwise I'll have to repeat it all later when I beg for your input as to how I'm supposed to handle this."

"You do know my input is pretty much worthless. I know nothing about health care and my only legal expertise is dealing with alleged criminals. Even that is suspect now."

"Why do you say that?"

"It's a long and complicated story."

Everything with her seemed to be, which made her all the more intriguing. "As I said before, you are a very mysterious woman."

"More like a beleaguered woman. I'll explain later. Alfred's problems get top billing now."

As if on cue, a nurse opened a door on the far side

of the room and called his name. "Ready or not, here we come," he muttered to no one in particular.

Rachel slipped her hand in his and squeezed. His spirits lifted. For what it was worth, it was nice having her on his side.

They were ushered into a small office with almost a dozen framed diplomas and other honors and acknowledgments hanging behind a large, neat desk. The man behind the desk looked to be in his midfifties, thin, with a receding hairline.

"I'm Dr. Riche," he said, extending a hand.

Luke shook it. "Luke Dawkins, and this is Rachel Maxwell."

The doctor shook Rachel's hand, as well. "Are you a relative of Alfred's, too?"

"No."

"She's a friend of mine," Luke explained quickly, "and an attorney, so feel free to speak honestly in front of her. Hopefully she'll guide me through any legal minefields we might run into in getting my dad the appropriate care."

"That could be useful before this is all over," the doctor affirmed, "though I won't be involved in that. My advice will strictly be medical except if you need medical information to support getting power of attorney. We have a lot to cover, so we might as well sit down and dive right in."

"That works for me," Luke said. "Just don't hit me

with a lot of medical terms I won't understand. I'm a basic fact kind of guy."

To his credit, the doctor did keep the professional terminology to a minimum, repeating what he'd told Luke on the phone the first time they talked about the type and possible causes of the stroke. He utilized an illustrated chart on his wall to further explain Alfred's atrial fibrillation and the possibilities for treating it.

"As I explained on the phone, your father's stroke was relatively mild and he should improve with the proper therapy, though he may not regain everything he's lost."

"What would that therapy entail?"

"He'll need to continue with the physical therapy to address the weakness on the left side of his body. In the meantime, he'll require a walker or a cane to help with balance and will continue to need a wheelchair for longer distances and uneven surfaces."

"Is he using a wheelchair now? He wasn't in one when I saw him Saturday."

"He refuses to use one most of the time, so someone must be with him anytime he walks more than a few feet. He is a very stubborn man."

"That I know. What else does he need in the way of therapy?"

"An occupational therapist can help with using eating utensils, bathing, opening jars and bottles, making himself a sandwich and other daily living skills. And he'll need a speech therapist, though some of his problems with finding the right word are closely related to his memory loss. We'll have to wait and see if that improves."

"Sounds like he could be in rehab for months."

"That won't be necessary. The social worker can help you set it up so that Alfred can get his therapy at home. But he will need someone with him. It could be months before he's capable of functioning totally on his own."

"Months?"

"Yes, but if all goes well, he'll be making progress during that time. The alternative to at-home care would be to put him in a long-term-care facility until he can function more independently."

"You mean like a nursing home?"

"Yes. There are facilities with differing levels of care so that a patient can move from one level to another as required."

"I'd have to hog-tie him to get him into one of those," Luke said, thinking out loud.

The doctor smiled. "And lock him in to keep him there."

"How long are we talking about before he can live on the ranch by himself with a minimum of help?"

"I'll be completely honest with you, Mr. Dawkins. I don't know how much of the ranch work your father was doing before the stroke, but he may never be able to do all the physical activities needed to fully run his ranch."

Luke felt as if he'd been slammed into a brick wall. Ranching was his father's life, more important than family had ever been to him.

Luke had resented that fact growing up. Now he couldn't help pitying his father.

"Alfred can go home with you as early as next week, or you can start making arrangements to put him in a long-term-care facility."

The walls began to close in around Luke. Letting Luke or anyone else take over Arrowhead Hills Ranch would finish what the stroke had started. It would completely destroy his father.

"I can't make that decision today," Luke said. "I'm not sure my father would consider letting me live at the ranch. We didn't part on good terms. Our only contact in years has been short phone calls initiated by me."

"That does complicate matters," Dr. Riche said. "Perhaps the social worker can help you sort out some of that. And luckily you have Rachel to help you with the legal issues, such as power of attorney for medical and financial issues."

Yeah. Just what Rachel needed. His problems heaped on top of hers.

He listened to the rest of what the doctor had to

say, but his mind was on Rachel instead of Alfred. He had no choice but to back out of her life while he dealt with the hell that had been dropped in his hands.

Alfred Dawkins had once again ruined his life.

RACHEL PICKED UP her pace to keep up with Luke as he practically ran across the parking lot and back to his truck. As upset as he was, he still stopped and opened her door for her. "Forgive my running off and leaving you back there. Guess I was trying to escape the inescapable."

"Been there," she said.

"I know. And now I feel like a rat for pulling you into my dilemma—not that it comes close to matching what you've been through."

"Maybe we shouldn't go and see Alfred just yet," she said as Luke started the engine and exited the parking garage. "You could probably use some time to look at the situation from different angles."

"Great idea," Luke agreed. "Another eleven years would help."

"I was thinking more like an hour or two."

"Lawyers are so rational. Are you hungry?"

"Not yet, and if your stomach is as tight as the way you're clutching the steering wheel, I doubt it would welcome food."

"No, but I could use a drink. It's almost noon. How about a margarita along the River Walk?"

"An excellent idea."

Traffic wasn't heavy and in less than a half hour, they'd driven to the center of the city, parked at one of the major hotels and made their way to the bustling waterway.

Visiting the River Walk always seemed like stepping into a new world to Rachel. Colorful umbrellas covered the waterside tables of a steady stream of restaurants.

Bright blooms in colorful pots were profuse even in January. Decorated boats filled with smiling people enjoying the view floated down the shallow river.

And music with a delightful Latin beat wafted through the air. It was the perfect place to spend a carefree January day, the blustery wind blocked by the city's skyscrapers, the noon sun making it seem more like spring than winter.

Unfortunately, this was anything but a carefree day for either of them. Rachel suspected that much of what Luke was feeling was heartache. Admittedly he'd never been close to his father, and now it might be too late to ever really know him.

Luke would have to dig deep to pull all that out and deal with it. She had no idea how to help him with that, especially with her own life in such a muddled and worrisome state.

They walked for a good ten minutes, stopping once to enjoy the music of a sidewalk mariachi band before finally checking out a less busy outdoor café attached to a hotel farther down the river. It was quieter here. Good for talking if he felt like it.

"How do those margaritas look to you?" he asked.

"Cool and refreshing."

It was the first time they'd spoken since leaving the parked car.

The hostess led them to a small table near the far side of the grouping of outdoor tables. They'd just ordered their drinks when Rachel's phone rang.

She checked the caller ID. It was Eric Fitch Sr. She killed the call.

"An unwanted admirer?" Luke teased.

"An unwanted ex-boss."

"Have you changed jobs recently?"

"You might say that."

"There you go with the mysterious explanations again."

The waitress returned with their drinks. She set them down, but instead of walking away she stared at Rachel. "You look just like the defense attorney whose picture was on television earlier. You know, the one who's defending Senator Covey's son."

"Do I? Sorry. Not my claim to fame," Rachel quipped.

"Good. That guy's guilty, sure as I'm standing here. That's how it is with those rich bastards. They think they can do anything they want and get away with it. It even has a name now. Affluenza or something like that."

"If he's guilty, hopefully he won't get away with it," Rachel said.

"He killed her, all right. He's evil. I've got a sense about these things, and soon as I saw him on television, I could see the evil in him."

An icy chill stitched itself around Rachel's heart. She turned away. Her breathing became difficult. An unconscionable reaction, considering she was getting this from a waitress who'd never met Hayden in person.

"Enjoy your drinks," the waitress said, oblivious to the anxiety churning inside Rachel. "No hurry. I'll take your food order when you're ready."

Rachel bit her bottom lip hard, needing the physical pain to override the panic attack.

Luke stretched his arms across the table and rested his hands on top of hers. "Your hands are cold as ice."

"I know. Give me a minute. I'll be okay." Her voice trembled.

"Don't let what the waitress said get to you. I can see how it would remind you of Roy Sales, but it doesn't mean anything."

"I know." Rachel gulped in a deep breath and exhaled slowly. "I'm the defense attorney the waitress was talking about," she admitted. "I saw that same evil in Hayden's eyes and I was only a few feet away from him."

"You're defending Hayden Covey?"

"That's to be determined at this point. I resigned from Fitch, Fitch and Bauman on Friday afternoon to avoid having to defend him. Eric Fitch Sr. is not used to being told no."

"Where do things stand now?"

"Somewhere between decayed and rotten. I thought my resignation had been accepted. Then Saturday night Senator Covey's wife was on the news announcing that Rachel Maxwell, who had been kidnapped and held hostage by the Lone Star Snatcher, was going to defend her son."

"She said all that, did she?"

"According to Sydney. I didn't hear it."

"Playing on the jury's sympathies even before the trial begins."

"You catch on fast."

"Gotta read the enemy if you want to stay alive."

"More marine rules?" she asked.

"Yep, and I'm alive. Proof it's a good rule. What are you going to do now?"

"Either go to the office and accept the sizable raise and offer of being named a junior partner Eric Fitch Sr. is blackmailing me with or call him and tell him what he can do with his offer. Essentially that equals wasting all the hard work I've put in for years and giving up my dream of one day being a partner with one of the most prestigious law firms in the state."

"You're dealing with all that today and yet you're here with me? Either you're a glutton for punishment or I'm one of the luckiest men around."

"You weren't feeling too lucky a few minutes ago," she reminded him.

"Everything is relative. Which way are you leaning?"

"It changes by the minute. My plan is to drive to Houston and see if some great revelation comes to me when I'm standing at the large glass double doors of Fitch, Fitch and Bauman."

"I'm going with you," he announced.

"You have Alfred to deal with."

"He's not going anywhere tomorrow. Neither is the ranch and I'm hiring help."

"That's fast."

"The wranglers were working for Adam McElroy before he sold off half his horses this past summer. Pierce highly recommends them, and that's good enough for me."

"For a man who claims to be a temporary cowboy, you are sure getting into the Western swing of things."

"It's growing on me. But I didn't mean to change the subject. Back to you."

"There is more," she admitted reluctantly. And no

real reason not to spill it all now that she was on a roll. She sipped her drink, appreciating the cold, tart liquid as it slid down her dry throat. "Dr. Kincaid has been calling my sister, Sydney, to get in touch with me."

"You lost me already. Who's Dr. Kincaid?"

"The lead psychiatrist in charge of Roy Sales's treatment."

"Why in hell would he call you?"

"Who knows? I'm guessing he thinks I know something that would help him pull Roy from his mental quagmire."

"Talk about gall. You don't owe him anything and you sure don't owe Roy Sales anything. Are you going to return his call?"

"Yes."

She didn't know that was her answer until it shot from her mouth. As much as she hated the thought of any involvement with Roy Sales, she needed to move on. Spending time these past three days with Luke had convinced her of that.

She hadn't died at Sales's torturous hand and she wouldn't let him win now. If she stayed trapped in the past, she'd lose the opportunity to truly live.

As crazy as she was about Luke, she knew he might not be her forever guy, but he'd awakened feelings inside her that she'd never expected to feel again.

Men like Luke wouldn't come along every day, but at least she knew they existed now.

"I doubt I have anything to say that would help Dr. Kincaid get Sales fit to stand trial any sooner," she explained, "but it's worth a chance."

She took a sip of her margarita and then took her phone from her handbag.

"You're going to call him right now?"

"Yes, before I change my mind." She punched in the doctor's phone number. Apparently it went to his private cell phone, since he took the call.

They barely got past the awkward small talk before he hurled the zinger.

"It's important that I observe Roy Sales interacting with you—in person."

Chapter Thirteen

Luke would have loved to hear Dr. Kincaid's side of the conversation, but he had to make do with Rachel's words and visible reactions. That was enough to know that the outcome of this call would not be good.

As if on cue, dark clouds began to roll in, hiding the sun and dropping the temperature a few degrees. Patrons at the tables around them finished their lunches quickly, paid their tabs and wandered off before they got caught in a storm.

The forecast was for a cold front to move in tonight, ushered in by heavy rain. This looked more like an afternoon thundershower. Unexpected changes in the weather were typical for this part of Texas.

But they should probably move on themselves to be on the safe side. Not that he'd hate getting caught in the rain with Rachel.

For that matter, doing anything with Rachel from scrubbing floors to having a water fight beat anything he'd done with anyone in recent memory.

It had been years since a woman affected him like this—if ever. He knew he was falling too fast and too hard, but logic had nothing to do with this. He'd lain awake for hours last night thinking of how she was messing with his mind and libido.

It was hard to be around her without touching her. Impossible to touch her and not want more. And kissing her literally left him aching to make love with her.

All in due time. When she was ready. When she wanted him the way he wanted her. God help him if that didn't come soon.

She finally broke the phone connection. "That was lovely," she said, her voice dripping satire.

"I got the feeling it might be. From what I heard it sounded like he wants you to come and talk to him in person."

"For starters. Then he wants me to talk to Roy Sales."

Luke muttered a few curses under his breath. "Surely you didn't agree to that."

"Not yet, but he's leaving an appointment open for me tomorrow morning in case I decide to cooperate."

"What does he expect to accomplish by putting you through that hell?"

"He thinks that Sales is either genuinely obsessed with me or else trying to play mind games with the doctor. He insists that it's all part of deciding if Sales is sane enough to stand trial."

"The psycho was so obsessed with you he tortured and tried to kill you."

"Yes, but either Roy doesn't remember or understand my captivity the way it was in actuality or he is manipulating the sessions. From what I know about him, I'd go with the latter."

"Exactly how does Sales remember it?"

"That I was with him willingly, that we shared an ethereal bond. Without a doubt he's mentally unbalanced, yet I'm convinced he was sane enough that he knew exactly what he was doing when he kidnapped me and the others. Sane enough that he knew to keep us hidden away and under lock and key."

"And that's sane enough to stand trial," Luke added.

"I definitely agree, and if my spending a few minutes with the monster can make that happen, it will be worth the emotional strain on me. I need this to be over once and for all."

"Then you plan to keep the appointment?"

"Unless I change my mind between now and tomorrow. I can stop at the mental facility on my way to Houston. It's not far out of the way."

"Sweetheart, you are piling it higher and higher on your plate. Are you sure you're up to this?"

"No. But I'm sure I need to do whatever it takes to get my life back. I don't expect to ever forget what Roy Sales put me through. I don't expect the nightmares to stop completely or to never have another panic attack."

She shoved her phone back in her purse and stood. "Talking about it with you was a breakthrough, but only a start. I have to keep pushing out the darkness so the light can come in."

"I have plenty of muscle power, courtesy of the marines. If you need any help pushing, count me in— for whatever you need."

"Then let's get started. No more talk of Roy Sales today. I want to think about music and flowers and the beautiful costumed girls who were dancing on the last boat that passed by. I want to think about walking in a field of clover and horseback riding across endless pastures and along bubbling creeks."

Luke walked over and tugged her up into his arms. "Anything else you want?"

"You. I want you, Luke Dawkins."

The first drops of rain began to pelt the umbrellas and the ledge, splashing raindrops on their heads and shoulders. Luke took her hand and they made a run for the restaurant door.

By the time they reached it, water was dripping from Rachel's hair and onto her forehead. He wiped it away with the palm of his hand.

The inside dining area was a few steps up a wide staircase and opened into a small but elegant boutique hotel.

"Would you like a table for two?" the hostess asked.

"Not just yet," Luke answered. "Give me a minute, Rachel. I'll be right back."

His heart hammered against his chest as he walked away. One should always give a lady what she wanted.

RACHEL LOOKED UP as Luke sauntered back across the room. He smiled and literally took her breath away. No man should look that good.

He handed her a hotel key.

"What is this?"

"Room service. We can dry off and eat comfortably."

"You rented a room for…"

She stopped midsentence as the gesture sank in slowly. She'd come on to him, said she wanted him. He'd taken her at her word and rented a room.

They were going to be alone. With a bed and crisp white sheets.

If that wasn't what she wanted, she'd best say so now.

Her pulse raced. She looked up, met his gaze and melted into it. She felt no fear or hesitancy. This was Luke Dawkins. A real man. A protector. A hero.

"I love room service," she whispered.

"Are you sure?"

"Never been surer in my life."

By the time they reached the room, she felt light-headed, the margarita and the anticipation both hitting her at once.

She stared at the bed, not afraid, but the moment was still awkward—until Luke wrapped her in his arms and covered her mouth in long, wet kisses that left her hungering for more.

He picked her up and carried her to the bed, shoved the coverlet out of the way and laid her between the soft cotton sheets. Luke pulled off her black booties and then kicked out of his boots and socks.

Standing next to the bed, he yanked his knit shirt over his head and dropped it onto a chair. His bronzed skin practically glowed in the dim light, the dark hairs on his chest all but hypnotizing as they narrowed into a V and disappeared into his jeans.

Desire swelled inside her, heating her insides and dancing along her nerves as he unzipped his jeans. He wiggled out of them. They fell to the floor. He kicked them away, leaving his clothes scattered around the room.

Even that was a turn-on.

He crawled into bed and stretched out beside her. His fingers fumbled with the buttons on her blouse. Her impulse was to help him, to hasten the moment his hands found her bare breasts and pebbled nipples. But she didn't want to miss one second of the foreplay for their first time together.

When they were both finally naked, his exploring fingers and sweet kisses trailed over her body.

She reached between them and took his erection in her hand.

"Now," she whispered. "I don't think I can wait another second."

"I don't want to hurt you, baby. You tell me if anything is too much and I'll pull back, I promise. I'd die before I hurt you."

Tears filled her eyes. Her body trembled with love. "You could never hurt me, Luke."

And he didn't. They came together in a rush of passion and pleasure that rocked her whole body.

When they got around to room service, it was perfect, too. They fed each other loaded nachos and washed the hot, spicy peppers down with another margarita.

"Perfection?" she asked when it was time to get dressed again.

"I'm not sure. I'll let you know after we try it a few thousand more times."

GOING FROM MIDDAY in heaven to an afternoon with his dad was as anticlimactic as one could get. But they'd driven here to see Alfred and his doctor, so he might as well get to the second part of his agenda.

It was four forty when Luke walked down the long hallway to Alfred's room. Rachel had excused herself to go to the ladies' room and to call Sydney. The sisters were close.

Luke couldn't see how anything good could come from Rachel's seeing Roy Sales again. If Sydney agreed with him, maybe she could talk some sense into Rachel.

Alfred's door was open. Luke tapped and then walked in. Alfred was in his hospital bed, the head raised until he was practically in a sitting position. The TV was on, but the volume was turned too low to make out what was being said.

Luke took off his slightly damp Stetson and tossed it onto an empty chair near the single narrow window.

"You look comfortable," he said. "How are you feeling?"

Alfred looked at him and then went back to staring at a rerun of *Home Improvement* on the muted TV.

Luke approached the foot of the bed. "Do you know who I am?"

"Yep."

"That's good. Did you have a good day?"

"Nope."

"We got some rain," Luke offered.

"Who's taking care—" Alfred hesitated, coughing before he finished the sentence "—care of the horses?"

"Your horses are in good hands. Pierce Lawrence

is seeing to that. He's helping me find wranglers and cowpunchers."

"Pierce."

"Yes. He said to tell you all is well at Arrowhead Hills."

"Good man."

"He is that."

Another tap on the open door. Luke turned and motioned Rachel to join them.

She smiled and walked over to stand next to Alfred. "Good afternoon, Mr. Dawkins."

A confused look settled on Alfred's face. "I took my...pills already. You a new...nurse?"

"I'm glad you took your meds. I'm not a nurse. I'm Rachel, a friend of Luke's."

"Humph."

"Luke talks about you all the time," she continued. "I'm so glad to finally meet you."

Alfred went back to staring at the TV.

"Don't let Luke sell my horses," he muttered, the rhythm of his words uneven. Apparently he was talking to Rachel, though he didn't look at her.

"Luke would never do that," Rachel answered. "He's taking good care of them. I visited your ranch. It's very nice."

"House is a mess."

"Not anymore," Luke said. "Rachel gave it a good cleaning."

"Luke helped," Rachel said.

"You like horses?"

"I do."

"Know how to ride?"

"I don't ride often, but I can stay in the saddle."

"I gotta go home. Horses need me."

"You have to get well first," Luke reminded him.

Alfred tried to push himself up on his elbows. His left elbow collapsed under him. Frustration deepened the wrinkles around his eyes and mouth.

Luke got a sick feeling deep in his gut. Alfred wasn't just ornery. He was also scared. Life as he knew it had been stolen by events he had no control over.

They might not have much of a father/son relationship, but Luke couldn't bear seeing him like this.

"Gotta get home," Alfred said again. "Horses need me."

"They do," Luke agreed. And Alfred desperately needed them. The decision Luke had expected to wrestle with for days had just made itself.

"I'm taking you home in a few days, Dad. I'll get everything ready and then I'll take you home. That's a promise."

Alfred turned away, but not before Luke saw the tears in his eyes.

"Your mama won't be there," Alfred said, his voice catching in a gruff sob.

Luke had no idea where that had come from, but his eyes grew moist, as well. Life took some bizarre turns.

Rachel walked over to Luke and squeezed his hand.

"I didn't know I had it in me," Luke muttered.

"I did."

The room grew silent until an aide entered with Alfred's dinner. Luke and Rachel introduced themselves.

"Does he always eat in his room?" Luke asked. "You must have a cafeteria of sorts."

"We have a great cafeteria. Alfred goes down for breakfast and lunch but insists he have dinner in his room. Don't you, Alfred?"

"Too much talking."

Luke wasn't sure if that meant it was difficult for him to talk and it wasn't worth the effort by the end of the day or that he'd had enough of people in general by then. Luke suspected it was a little of both.

When the aide left, Rachel handed Alfred the wet cloth to wash his hands and then opened his carton of milk, stuck the straw into it and arranged his tray so that he could get to everything easily.

Alfred smiled appreciatively. No doubt he liked Rachel. But then, who wouldn't?

"We should go and let you eat while it's hot," Luke said.

"Not..." He hesitated. "Never hot," Alfred complained as he shoved a spoonful of mashed potatoes into his mouth.

A bit spilled from his mouth and landed on his shirt. He didn't seem to notice.

Rachel wiped the blob of food from his shirt with a napkin and spread his napkin under his chin to catch any additional mishaps.

They were practically out the door when Alfred's angry yell got their instant intention.

"Murderer."

"What did you say?" Luke asked.

"Murderer." He pointed his spoon at the TV.

Luke checked it out. The five o'clock news had come on and the Breaking News warning was splashed across the screen with the picture of Hayden Covey just below it.

Rachel grabbed the remote and turned up the volume.

The judge had set Hayden Covey's bail at one million dollars.

Luke let out a low whistle. "That's a lot of cash for a schoolboy."

"He's twenty. That's not a schoolboy in the legal system. A million dollars is not out of line for someone arrested for murder."

"Guess it doesn't matter in his case," Luke said.

"His father will come up with it. How does that affect your resignation?"

"If Eric has already replaced me with the attorney who arranged for bail, then I'm definitely in the market for a new job."

Which wouldn't be bad in Luke's mind, but he wasn't counting that a done deal yet.

Rachel's mind was whirling as Luke pulled in behind Sydney's car. For four months, she'd felt trapped in a time warp, trying to block everything to do with Roy Sales from her mind, only to be faced with her fears at every turn.

She'd passed some kind of milestone in a few days, pulled her abduction and captivity from the dark crevices of her mind and exposed them to the stark light of reality. Now she was about to face Roy Sales straight on. Weirdly, she felt more emboldened than afraid.

Luke killed the engine and reached for her hand. "Are you sure I can't persuade you to go home with me tonight?"

"No, but you get points for making it hard to say good-night. Thanks for a memorable day."

"No reason we can't top that off with an even more memorable night."

"That is the most tempting offer of my life, but seriously, I need to spend some time with Sydney. I'd like her input on meeting with Sales and Eric Fitch.

And you have a ranch to run now that you've officially made the decision to stay at Arrowhead Hills. At least, I think that's what you meant when you promised to take your dad home."

"I did, though it may turn out to be the biggest mistake of my life."

"It was the right thing to do."

"Keep telling me that when I start to rip my hair out and run around wildly in circles."

"I will. I'm sure Esther has some leftovers from dinner if you're hungry."

"No. I'm good. Pierce said Esther had him deliver a food basket to the ranch today. He claims it's enough food to last me till spring."

"When did you talk to Pierce?"

"While you were drying your hair back at the hotel. I had high hopes then for not making it back to the ranch tonight. To be honest, I had hopes for not making it back for days."

"I don't think a good cowboy would ever shirk his job to mess around," she teased.

"You've got a lot to learn about cowboys. Afternoon delight with a beautiful woman trumps wrangling every time."

He let go of her hand and opened the door.

"You don't have to walk me to the door," she said.

"I know, but I have to kiss you good-night properly, or better yet, improperly."

He rounded the truck quickly and opened her door.

"Are you sure you want to drive me to Houston tomorrow? You really do have a lot of work to do. And they're forecasting storms for tonight and early morning."

"The work will get done with or without me. Buck Stallings is going to give the new wranglers a trial run for the rest of the week. Dudley Miles says he can spare even more cowpunchers if I need them. Barring the unexpected, January is a relatively quiet time in the ranching business."

"It might be storming."

"Then we'll leave a little later. Call me when you're ready to leave. No way am I letting you face Roy Sales alone."

He pulled her into his arms. The kiss was improper enough that she was weak-kneed and dizzy with desire by the time she made it to the porch.

Sydney met her at the door, a worried look on her face.

"What's wrong?" Rachel asked.

"You have company."

"Who?"

"Claire Covey. She's bordering on hysterical and says it's urgent that she talk to you."

Chapter Fourteen

Rachel stepped into the small office at the end of the hall that Esther used for clipping and organizing coupons and for keeping up with the church and community organizations she enjoyed so much. It consisted of a desk, an office chair, a bookcase and a comfortable accent chair near the one narrow window.

Claire was waiting, standing near the desk. She wasn't hysterical at the moment, but her eyes were red and swollen and a pile of tissues lying on the desk beside her were ripped to shreds.

Except for the red and swollen eyes, Claire was an attractive woman, likely somewhere in her early forties. Her short blond hair was cut into a stylish pageboy.

Her slacks and sweater were classic but had that designer edge to them that shouted money. The handbag on the floor beside her chair was Gucci.

"I'm Rachel Maxwell. How can I help you?"

"I know who you are. I know all about you and

what you've been through. I don't know how you endured it."

"It was difficult, but I'm sure that's not what brought you here tonight."

"I need your help. The police are pinning a murder on my son. He's innocent, but that doesn't matter to them. They won't listen to reason. All they want is to send him to prison."

Claire burst into tears and buried her face in her hands as sobs shook her body.

Rachel gave her a minute to regain a semblance of composure. She could understand Claire's fears. She was a mother who loved her son. "Do you believe Hayden is innocent?"

"I know he's innocent. He would never hurt anyone. Never. The girl was after him, calling him all hours of the night, and then he'd see her out with other guys."

Blaming the victim was a common counter, but it seldom led anywhere. "You should probably be discussing this with your attorney."

"That was supposed to be you," Claire said. "Eric Fitch promised us it would be you. The jury will believe you if you tell them he's innocent. You'd never defend a monster. Not after what you've been through."

"The jury would be right," Rachel agreed. "I'd never defend an accused murderer unless I was convinced he was innocent. But defending a case involves a lot more than just connecting with the jury."

"Eric said you were an extremely talented defense attorney, the best chance of Hayden being acquitted."

"Eric may have exaggerated that a bit. Exactly when did Eric tell you that I wouldn't be handling your case?"

"This afternoon. He called about two and said you'd left the firm for personal reasons, but I'm begging you, please don't turn your back on Hayden. Don't let them ruin his life. Don't let them take my son."

Her words cracked into sobs.

Rachel wondered if Eric had changed his mind about wanting her back or if he was just covering the odds. Was he trying to make sure that he didn't lose the Coveys as clients if Rachel didn't come back?

"Who arranged the bail?" Rachel asked.

"Eric. He wants to be the lead attorney," Claire explained.

"Eric does have a lot of influence in this state. It's doubtful anyone else could have done that so quickly if at all," Rachel said, giving him his due.

"I don't care about his influence. I don't care about my husband's reputation. I don't care about anything except my boy. I'll get on my knees if it will help. I'll pay you any amount of money you want. Just please save my boy."

Claire's pain seemed to cut right into Rachel's heart. Like all mothers, she was no doubt prejudiced, but that didn't mean she was wrong. Rachel had judged Hayden on one look, but that might have been colored by her own fears.

"Just talk to Hayden," Claire begged. "You'll see he could never have killed anyone. You'll see the goodness in him. I know you will."

It was hard to say no to that simple request.

"I'll meet with him. That's all I can promise. Even if I decide to take Hayden's case, I may not be doing it in conjunction with Eric's firm."

"I don't care."

"But there could be legal and ethical issues that apply to my taking a case from Fitch, Fitch and Bauman so soon after my resignation."

"It's my son's future that's at stake," Claire begged. "What could be unethical about that?"

"Does your husband agree with you on moving the case from the law firm?"

"He'll do what I say."

If she took Hayden's case, her plate wouldn't just be piled high as Luke said. It would spill over and pool at her feet like acid rain. "When do you expect Hayden to be released on bail?"

"Hopefully tomorrow, but Eric said it could take days."

"I'm driving to Houston in the morning and I'll

likely be there until Wednesday afternoon. If Hayden is released before that, give me a call and we can set up an appointment for me to meet with Hayden. The meeting will likely not be at Fitch's law firm."

"I'll bring him wherever you say—whenever you want."

"Good. We can decide that later."

Tears filled Claire's eyes again. She sniffled and grabbed a new tissue. "You can't imagine what this means to me."

Rachel could imagine, but she couldn't let this decision be ruled by emotions. Murder was not a game of hearts. "I hope I can help, Claire. I sincerely hope I can deliver what you're asking, but remember, all I'm agreeing to now is a meeting with Hayden. We'll see where it goes from there."

When Claire stood to go, she trembled, and for a second Rachel thought she might pass out. Rachel extended an arm for support and Claire leaned against her, her head resting on Rachel's shoulder.

Rachel hoped beyond hope that Hayden was the young man his mother believed him to be. But deep down in Rachel's soul, she had the grievous feeling that he wasn't.

RACHEL HAD SHOWERED and changed into a pair of pink flannel pajamas by the time Sydney joined her in her bedroom. Sydney was dressed in jeans and a sapphire-colored sweater.

"Sorry to be so late, but I was painting Esther's toenails for her. She thinks shop pedicures are a waste of money. Besides, I thought you might need some time to regroup after Claire Covey left."

"I don't know that it helped."

"Want to start from the top with Claire Covey?"

Rachel fed her the details.

"Eric Fitch is going explode when he hears you lured the highest-profile case of the decade."

"I didn't lure."

"You'll never convince him of that."

"Does that mean you think I shouldn't take the Covey case?"

"No. It means I hate to miss the blowup when he gets what he deserves for trying to manipulate and then blackmail you."

"It wasn't quite that bad."

"It is from my point of view. Do you think you'll run into legal hassles?"

"My contract was renewed a little over a year ago. A friend from law school specializes in contract law. She reviewed the contract and I'm certain she didn't let me sign anything overly constrictive at that point in my career."

"I guess the legalese would matter. I mean, if it says you can't start your own firm and lure away his clients, that wouldn't cut it in this case, would it? You're not opening your own firm and you didn't lure her from him. Claire Covey came to you."

"True to a point. The most pressing question may come down to, do I really want to defend a young man I just gave up a prosperous career position over so that I didn't have to defend him?"

"That's a tongue twister," Sydney said. "But you didn't actually resign because Eric asked you to take a case you didn't want."

"True. I resigned because I was being used. At the time, money and promotions had nothing to do with my decision."

"Do you want to defend Hayden Covey?" Sydney asked.

"Not unless I can believe in his innocence. The murder was brutal. I get sick just reading about it."

"I'll see what I can find out about the crime, though the FBI is not involved. I checked."

"Anything would help."

"I wish I could hang around with you for a few more days and keep up with your continuing saga, but I have to cut my minivacation even shorter. I'm needed in Wisconsin asap for an important investigation. All hush-hush."

"Okay, now I'll worry about you instead of me."

"Please don't. I've got the FBI behind me, and it doesn't get any safer than that."

Rachel wasn't convinced that was always true. "Not to try to outdo you, but I have other news, as well. I'm seeing Dr. Kincaid and Roy Sales tomorrow."

"I don't like the sound of this," Sydney lamented. "I can understand talking to the doctor, but why Roy Sales? I wouldn't have told you the doctor called if I'd known he was going to ask that of you."

"Sure you would have. You're a stickler for the truth and we always level with each other. Besides, if it helps get Sales to trial, it will be worth it."

"Not necessarily. At any rate, if things get too harried in Houston, you can always come to Winding Creek for a rest. Esther would love to have you. So would the rest of the family."

"Actually, I'll be staying in Houston only one night."

"Really? Does this have anything to do with Luke Dawkins?"

"He's driving me to Houston. He wants to be there when I talk to Roy Sales. He thinks I may need a little moral support for that and for my talk with Eric if I decide to meet with him."

"That's generous of him and probably a good idea."

"He's a genuine guy."

"I don't doubt that. I just worry that with all that's

going on in your life right now, is this the best time to fall into a serious relationship?"

"Is there ever a good time to fall into a relationship?"

"Some might be better than others."

"Was it the right time when you met Tucker? His best bull-rider friend had just been killed in competition. You were trying to find and rescue me from a monster."

"Point made. Tucker and I didn't find love. It found us. We were just smart enough to listen to our hearts."

"I'm just taking this one day as at a time," Rachel said, "but I like him and I like being with him. That feels really good right now."

More than good and she more than liked him. And she couldn't wait to make love with him again. That part she wouldn't share with Sydney.

"Don't worry about me, Sydney. I'm not fully healed. I may never be, but I'm making progress. You and Tucker saved my life. I'm planning to make the most of it, and right now that includes Luke."

"Got it. Just keep me posted—about Sales and Hayden Covey. And what you decide about your job."

"I will, but I'm definitely leaning toward leaving the firm."

"Take that job and shove it. I'm with you all the way. There's more to life than work. Try it. You might like it."

"You're a fine one to talk, but I may just do that."

"I'm really glad we had this time together," Sydney said.

"Me, too. Luke and I didn't set a time to leave in the morning, but I doubt I'll be leaving before you get up."

"Unfortunately, I'm leaving—" Sydney glanced at her watch "—in about thirty minutes. I have to catch an early flight to Kansas and Tucker wasn't ready to say goodbye, so we booked a hotel near the airport for the night. He'll see me off and head out a day early for his next competition."

"Then I guess this is goodbye." Rachel pulled Sydney into a hug. "Stay safe," she whispered.

"That's the plan. You be careful and call me if you need to talk about anything. And forget what I said about your relationship with Luke. If he makes you happy, that's all that matters. I love you, sis."

"I love you, too."

And the good part was they always would.

ROY SALES WATCHED as Eddie cracked his knuckles and then stuck his index finger into his water glass like it was a straw.

"Get your finger out of your water," Doug the crank complained. "You've got no manners."

"Don't need them in this place," Eddie said. "I'm

leaving here any day now. My son's got a yacht down in the Gulf. He wants me to come live with him."

"Sure he does," Roy said. "I'll come down and visit you."

"You wouldn't like it. My boy Rick don't allow no drinking or smoking. He don't even cuss."

"Then why go there?" Doug asked. "You might as well go to jail."

"Jail's for jerks," Eddie said.

Roy smiled. Any other time, Doug and Eddie would be getting on his nerves so bad he'd have gone back to his room and read another paperback Western.

He never thought he'd say it, but he missed working for Dudley Miles. Work was hard sometimes, but he had a lot of freedom and a house of his own.

He wouldn't be going back to Dudley's, but he wouldn't be leaving Texas just yet. He had one little detail left over from his life here to take care of.

Killing Rachel Maxwell wasn't just for fun. It was necessary if he was going to even the score. A real man had to even the score.

Doug Crank was going on and on now about the fact that they didn't ever get a decent steak. That was the damn truth, but it wouldn't matter much longer to Roy.

He'd played the game like a championship boxer going for the knockout punch. He'd figured out fast who could help him and how to make sure they would.

The pawns were all in place. It was only a matter of time. Maybe tomorrow. By next week, for sure.

First he'd take care of business and then he'd get his steak.

He looked up and saw Dr. Kincaid walking toward him. Something must be up. Kincaid never came around this late in the day.

"Good evening," the doc said, approaching the group of three.

"You working overtime?" Eddie asked.

"No, I'm here to talk to Roy. Would you two mind giving us a few minutes alone?"

"We can go to my room," Roy said, not that it was much of a room, but it was still nicer than any bunkhouse he'd ever slept in. He had a nice bed with clean chairs and a soft pillow. There was even a chest and a small desk. The chair wasn't so much, but it was good enough.

The doc followed him to his room. Roy sat on the edge of the bed and the doc took the chair. "I'm not in trouble, am I? That yelling fight at lunch wasn't my fault."

"You're not in trouble. In fact, I have a surprise for you."

Roy didn't bite. He just waited to see what the doc had to say.

"You're having a visitor tomorrow."

That was a shocker. The only visitors he'd had

since he'd been here were unfriendly reporters and his jerk of an attorney, and they weren't allowed in often.

"Aren't you going to ask who?" Kincaid asked.

"I figure you're going to tell me or you wouldn't be here."

"You're right. Rachel Maxwell is stopping by tomorrow."

Roy swallowed hard. That was the last person he'd expected. "What does she want?"

"I asked her to come."

Roy should have known this wasn't Rachel's idea.

"You're always telling me how the two of you bonded. I figured you'd enjoy seeing her."

"Yeah, well, you never know about women. She wanted to run away with me, but she lied about that to the police and she'll probably lie about it again."

"Maybe she won't. Anyway, I thought I'd prepare you for her visit so you wouldn't be too surprised when she shows up."

"Are you going to be with us in the room when we talk?"

"Do you want me to be?"

"Suit yourself."

"We'll talk about those arrangements tomorrow with Rachel."

The doc blabbered on a few minutes and then left.

Roy kicked off his shoes and stretched out on the bed. Rachel Maxwell was coming here. She probably felt bad about all those lies she told about him. He wasn't that bad. She'd wanted him to come around and always wanted him to stay longer. But then when he had his back against the wall, she'd turned on him.

She'd left him no choice but to leave her to burn to death in the fire.

He tried to remember what she looked like the day he first saw her in downtown Winding Creek. All that hair catching the sun and shining like gold. Great eyes. He'd never seen eyes as beautiful as hers.

He hadn't wanted to hurt her so bad, but she kept fighting him.

He didn't want to kill her now, but she'd betrayed him. In the end, she'd treated him like a monster, the way the others had.

"What should I do, Mommy?"

"Wait and see. We just have to wait and see."

Chapter Fifteen

Light rain pattered on the roof as Rachel fell into a troubled sleep. She woke to a blazing streak of lightning that lit up her bedroom like a flashing neon sign. A thunderous bolt of thunder that shook the windows followed a second later.

It was pitch-dark outside until the next light show created an eerie shadow dance on her wall.

Rachel shivered and reached for the extra quilt on the foot of the bed. Evidently the promised cold front had arrived with the storm. From short sleeves to jackets in a matter of hours and then back to shorts again within days. That was Texas weather.

She'd just snuggled under the extra covers again when she got a whiff of coffee. The storm must have wakened Esther, too, though she was always up with the rooster's first crow. She claimed the big, noisy bird that Grace swore had it in for her was the only alarm clock she could always count on.

Esther loved her chickens. The fresh eggs were just a bonus.

Rachel reached for her phone and checked the time. Ten after five. She looked a second time to be sure she'd seen that right.

Seven hours straight of sound sleep and she might still be asleep if not for the storm. She hadn't slept that long since...

Since Roy Sales with his tortured brand of misery had forced himself into her life.

And now she'd agreed to interact with him again. Agreed to stare into his cold, heartless eyes and get another glimpse of his dark soul. She had a growing fear that she might live to regret this.

Rachel swallowed hard, kicked off the covers and slid her feet to the soft rug as the nauseating memories began to haunt her mind yet again. Only this time, she wouldn't give in to the terror.

Luke had been the catalyst who helped her bring everything into the open. They were friends and lovers, but she wasn't so naive that she was convinced what they had would last forever. She didn't need a promise of forever.

What they shared was enough for now.

Rachel padded to the window in her bare feet and opened the blinds. Rain pelted the windows, the water falling in sheets. Hopefully the storm would pass before they had to leave for Houston. It wouldn't be safe driving in this. Sydney and Tucker had been smart to leave the night before.

Wide-awake, she grabbed a robe and gave in to the lure of the smell of coffee. She heard male voices. Surely Luke hadn't shown up this early and in the peak of the storm.

When she reached the kitchen, she saw that it was Pierce and a young man she didn't recognize, both in their work clothes as if this was just another ranching day.

Pierce turned toward her and tipped his steaming coffee mug. "Good morning, Rachel. Hope we didn't wake you."

"The storm beat you to it. Is something wrong? Are Jaci and Grace okay?"

"They're fine, though Grace didn't sleep much last night. Between the storm, going to the bathroom and trying to find some way to get comfortable, she tossed half the night."

Esther poured another mug of coffee and handed it to Rachel. "I don't know if you've met Buck Stallings," she said, nodding toward the other man in the room.

"I've heard his name from Luke," she said, "but no, I haven't met him."

"Buck's only the hardest working wrangler in the county," Pierce said. "And the closest thing I've ever seen to what I'd call a real horse whisperer."

"Don't buy that tall tale," Buck said. "Most of what I know I've learned from Pierce over the last year."

Esther shook her head. "Don't neither one of you seem to have the sense God gave a goose this morning. No good reason I can see for you two to get out in this weather. It's not like the cows need you to bring them a slicker."

"Horses are likely riled," Buck said. "A soft voice, a couple of pats and some fresh hay to chew on will settle them down a bit."

"You'll be back for a hot breakfast, won't you?" Esther asked. "I'm thinking fried chicken and waffles."

"You do know how to tempt a guy, but I can't make any promises," Pierce said. "It all depends on what we run into. I've got a few pastures I need to check. Drainage is improved, but it hasn't been tested like this."

"You need hot food," she mumbled, obviously reluctant to give up the argument. He and Buck were already pulling on their jackets.

"I'm hoping Grace went back to sleep for another hour or so. If I'm not back by seven, can one of you give Grace a call just to make sure she's okay and see if she needs any help getting Jaci up and ready for school? Not that I expect you to get out in the storm, but call me if you think she needs me and I'll get back her on the double."

"Of course we will," Esther said. "Would have done that even if you hadn't asked. I don't care if the doctor did say she had another two weeks to go. That son of yours is about to kick himself into the world."

"I know Grace hopes you're right. You two stay warm and dry." Pierce gave Esther a peck on the check and he and Buck headed toward the back door.

Esther went after them and pushed a large thermos of hot coffee into Pierce's hand. "Be careful," she said.

"Always. And like I said, if you think for a minute Grace needs me, call."

"You bet your best past pair of spurs I will."

"I can't believe they're going out in this weather," Rachel said when the door shut behind them.

"It's the ranching life," Esther said. "Living with my Charlie for fifty-two years, I learned that the livestock comes first. You get used to it, honey. Fact is, I wouldn't have changed it for life in a golden tower. I sure wouldn't change it for city life where you're lucky to even know your neighbors.

"Not that I'm faulting your life, Rachel. The world needs good lawyers, too. It just wouldn't be the life for me."

"There are days I'm not sure it's the life for me."

This was one of those days, but Rachel was doubtful she'd fit into this life, either.

Another bolt of lightning sizzled across the sky.

This time the thunder was so loud the house felt like a giant was shaking it.

Rachel wondered if Luke was out in the storm, checking on livestock this morning. If so he was no doubt regretting that he'd offered—no, insisted—to drive her to Houston today. Like Esther said, livestock comes first.

Rachel's life was in Houston. Luke's was here, at least for the time being. She couldn't imagine the two lifestyles meshing.

Only, unless she and Eric Fitch Sr. came to an agreement, she didn't exactly have a lifestyle or a career.

And work was the only life she knew.

AN HOUR LATER, the sky had grown lighter and the thunder rumbled in the distance instead of shaking the house. The rain was still falling steadily, with bursts of monsoon-level intensity. If this kept up, she might have to delay her trip to Houston until tomorrow.

Rachel bypassed the dark gray suit she had planned to wear and instead chose a pair of chocolate-colored slacks and a wine-colored sweater.

She pulled on a pair of brown, flat-heeled leather boots that had previously encountered mud puddles and proven their survival skills. She'd need to pick up additional clothing at her apartment if she planned to stay in Winding Creek through the following weekend.

Any longer than that would definitely be taking advantage of Esther's hospitality.

Rachel found Esther in the kitchen, shelling pecans into a small bowl that was already half-full. "There's a fresh pot of coffee," Esther said.

"Thanks. Have you heard from Grace?"

"No, but I'm sure she's up. This is the worst gully washer we've had in years. I do remember one June, though, when I thought we were going to wash plumb away. Charlie joked he was building an ark and swatting the mosquitoes before it started floating so he wouldn't be saving them."

Rachel poured herself a cup of coffee. "Hopefully we won't reach ark stage this time, but I do like his mosquito extermination program."

There was a loud banging at the back door followed by the sound of stamping feet.

"About time Pierce got back here," Esther said. She dropped the cracked pecan in the basket.

But when the door opened, it was Luke, not Pierce, who was standing there. The gray slicker he was wearing pooled on the mat. His boots were caked in mud despite the stamping.

Esther grabbed the nearest dish towel and rushed to the door. "Sakes alive, Luke, you look like you fell into Winding Creek and stayed for a fish dinner."

"Feel like it, too," he agreed. "Never mind the towel. I'm too big a mess to come in."

"Of course you can come in. That's what mops are for."

"I can just stay a minute." He stepped inside and onto the indoor mat.

"Is something wrong?" Rachel asked.

"I got a call from Pierce. He says there's been a mudslide out near the gorge. It took part of the fence line with it."

Esther covered her mouth with both hands as if holding in an exclamation. "Are the cattle okay?"

"Most of them. Some of the young cows have gotten tangled in the downed barbwire or stuck in the mud. Three or four have slid partway into the gorge. Pierce and Buck have their hands full, so I came to help."

"Did they call Riley?" Esther asked.

"Riley's on his way. He's bringing his own four-wheeler, since there's no way to get a truck to that area without getting it stuck. Pierce says there's another four-wheeler in the barn."

"There is," Esther said. "The key's in it. There should be some ropes in there, as well."

"I brought some with me. Pierce just wanted me to let you know what's going on so you didn't worry when he doesn't show up for breakfast. And he wants someone to let Grace know what's going on. He said try not to upset her."

"I'll get you a thermos of coffee to take with you and a few tea cakes. You guys will need something to warm your insides and give you energy."

Rachel walked over to the door while Esther prepared the treats.

"I'm sorry about this," Luke said. "I'm not sure how long this is going to take, but I don't want you going to Houston without me."

"Don't worry about me. I'll be fine," she assured him.

"That's not the answer I'm looking for. I don't want you facing that sick son of a bitch alone. Promise me you aren't making that trip without me or I'm not leaving here."

He was worried and protective. And caring. Her heart caved. "I promise, Luke. Now go, cowboy. You have cows to rescue." He kissed her hard on the mouth. Possessive, as if they belonged to each other.

Esther handed him the thermos and a plastic tote full of disposable cups and the cake-like sugar cookies as he left. Into the storm and the frosty temperatures.

Pierce needed him and he was eager to help. There was little room for doubt now. The odds were good that he was a rancher at heart.

And that she was too crazy about him for words.

"No use to cook breakfast for the men," Esther said. "It will be lunchtime or later before we see them again."

"Do you really think it will take that long?"

"I s'pect it will. Not fretting about it. Livestock and the land. That's a rancher's lifeblood. I can't tell you how many plans of mine got canceled over the years because of an animal emergency."

"You must have gotten annoyed with that on occasion."

"Would've been a big, fat waste of time if I did. Besides, I knew my Charlie loved me. Deep down, I was proud of how responsible he was. Made me feel safe."

Safe.

That was how Luke made Rachel feel. Safe. She'd forgotten how it felt until Luke had come along.

"I can whip up some bacon and eggs for the two of us in no time or I can make us a nice peach cobbler from the summer fruit I froze. Some folks don't like cobbler for breakfast, but I say if it's good, time of day don't matter."

"Please don't go to that trouble for me. Toast is fine, especially topped off with some of your home-made fig preserves."

"That sounds mighty good to me, too, along with a tall glass of milk."

Rachel put two slices of artisan bread from Dani's

bakery in the toaster and set the table while Esther got out the preserves, butter and milk.

"It sure was nice having Tucker and Sydney here this weekend," Esther said as they sat down across from each other in the breakfast nook. "Having you here, too, made it extraspecial."

"I hope I'm not wearing out my welcome."

"Don't you ever worry about that. Does an old woman good not to wander around a big house like this all alone every night. Not that I don't have plenty of family, but there's always room for one more if they're nice as you."

"Thank you."

"What do you think of the Dawkins boy?"

Rachel didn't think of Luke as a boy, but Esther had her own way of saying things. "He's very nice."

"He was a good kid, too. Me and his mama were best friends before she died. She was a good twenty years younger than me, but we just hit it off right from the day we met."

"How old was Luke when she died?"

"A couple of years older than Jaci is now, around eight, I suspect. Luke was her heart from the day he was born. He was all that mattered to her. Broke her heart when she walked away and left him behind."

"Why did she leave him?"

"She didn't leave him. She left Alfred. I think he

was a good man deep down, but he was controlling and ornery."

"Alfred must have been a lot older than her."

"He was, but he was a good-looking man with a lot going for him. He adored her and she loved him at first."

"What happened?" Rachel asked.

"He was jealous and that brought out the worst in him. He didn't want her to leave the house and got too crotchety to bear. She was like a butterfly, flitting around, bringing beauty and light to everything and everyone she touched."

"Everyone except Alfred?"

"I reckon he was so afraid of losing her that he eventually ran her off. Before she got settled and came back for Luke, she got killed in a head-on collision."

Esther picked up the napkin and dabbed her eyes. "I swear I can't think of that day without getting all weepy."

That explained why Luke felt the way he did about his dad. He probably blamed him for losing his mother. Yet he'd come home to take care of his father when Alfred needed him.

Luke Dawkins was an amazing man.

RACHEL TOOK ADVANTAGE of a slowdown in the rain to make the ten-minute drive to Pierce and Grace's cabin. The old blacktop ranch road gave way to a long, curving gravel drive for the last fifty yards. Driving was slick and water flowed like a river along the eastern edge of the road.

There was no garage, but Pierce and his brothers had built a covered carport that provided a dry, mud-free path to the back door. Rachel parked, walked to the door and knocked. The damp, cold air chilled her to the bone. Her black waterproof trench coat would have felt good, but it was back in Houston.

Jaci opened the door and did a twirl to show off her new yellow-flowered raincoat with matching yellow boots. Even the opened umbrella matched.

"You look like you're going out dancing in the rain."

"I wanted to, but Mommy won't let me. Like, what's the point of having a new raincoat if I can't get out in the rain?"

She twirled again as if that would make her point.

"You don't want to get those boots all wet, do you?" Rachel asked.

"Well, a girl's gotta do what a girl's gotta do. That's what my cousin Constance says."

"But you, young lady, have to do what Mommy and Daddy say," Grace reminded her. "And we say it's much too cold and wet to be jumping into mud puddles, especially before school."

Jaci's hands went to her hips, but then she quickly went back to regaling them with her dance routine.

Grace fell back into one of the kitchen chairs. She looked pale and frail.

"How are you feeling?" Rachel asked.

"Tired. I'm at that stage in the pregnancy where a good night's sleep would be more exciting than winning the lottery."

"That's tired," Rachel agreed. And it showed in Grace's face and the stoop to her shoulders. Her ready smile was nowhere to be seen.

"Have you had breakfast?" Rachel asked.

"I ate a few bites of yogurt, but I have no appetite this morning."

That didn't sound like a good thing to Rachel, but she wasn't going to push food on Grace when she didn't feel like eating. "What about Jaci? Has she had breakfast?"

"I had a peanut butter sandwich and it was yummy," Jaci said, jumping into the conversation.

"It's what she wanted," Grace said, "and I didn't have the energy to argue with her. I figure peanut butter and jelly is as good for her as those sugary cereals she likes so much."

"Sounds healthy enough to me," Rachel agreed.

She was far more worried about Grace's health. If you'd asked Rachel yesterday, she would have sworn the one thing consuming her thoughts this morning would have been the impending meeting with Roy Sales.

Now she was seriously worried about Grace, and cows and the men taking care of them. She was also concerned that she was becoming so involved in this life that she really didn't want to go to Houston today without Luke.

"Perhaps you should call your obstetrician," Rachel said, "just to be on the safe side. You don't want to come down with a virus this close to your due date."

"I will if I don't feel better soon, but I think I'm just tired. One decent night's sleep would work miracles."

"My little brother is growing in Mommy's tummy," Jaci said. "That's why she's getting so fat." Jaci put down her umbrella and patted Grace's stomach. "I'll be a big sister."

"That is very exciting," Rachel said. "Would you like me to drive you to the gate to wait on your school bus?"

"Yes. Can she, Mommy?"

"Absolutely, but the bus won't be here for about twenty more minutes. Why don't you go and practice this week's new words until it's time to go?"

"I don't need practice. I already know them all. But I could go work on my coloring. Art is my favorite subject."

She skipped off, leaving Rachel and Grace alone.

"You're going to have your hands full with Jaci and the baby. Are you ready for it?"

"To tell you the truth, it scares me to death. Jaci and I have bonded so beautifully and I don't want to lose any of that. Still, I know the baby is going to require a lot of my time. Pierce keeps trying to reassure me, but I worry that Jaci will feel left out."

"You'll have a lot of help," Rachel said. "This family seems to stick together in everything."

"You're right about that. It would be supernice if you lived closer. You may need a lot more time unwinding on the back of a horse if you're really going to represent Hayden Covey."

"So you heard about that?"

"Everyone has. It was on the news all day yesterday. The family just doesn't want you to think they're butting into your business, so they won't ask about it until you mention it."

"The news media have jumped the gun. The decision hasn't been made as to whether or not I'll defend him."

Grace started to get out of the chair but winced in pain and grabbed her side.

Rachel panicked. "Was that a labor pain?"

"I don't think so. I was just at the doctor's yesterday. He said it would likely be at least another week, maybe two."

"Is that the first pain like that you've had?"

"The second," Grade admitted. "I had one when I first got out of bed this morning."

"I know next to nothing about labor pains," Rachel admitted, "but I think you should call your doctor or at least call Esther."

"I will if..."

Grace stopped talking and stood perfectly still as water began to run down her legs and pool around her feet. "I think my water just broke."

"Call your doctor." This time Rachel ordered instead of suggesting. "I'm calling Esther and she can call Pierce."

Esther was at the door only a minute or two after Grace got off the phone with her doctor's nurse.

"They want me to come in now," Grace said.

"I can drive you," Rachel said.

"That's what Pierce suggested, as well," Esther said. "He'll meet you there as fast as he can get back here and scrape off some of the mud."

"Can you drive Jaci to the school bus stop?" Grace asked Esther.

"Of course I can."

Minutes later, Grace and Rachel were in the car driving to the hospital. Grace was having her baby.

Roy Sales and even Eric Fitch would just have to wait. The biggest drama of life couldn't.

Chapter Sixteen

Luke arrived at Esther's house to pick up Rachel before eight o'clock on Wednesday morning. Every muscle in his body ached from the hours they'd spent saving a few cows yesterday.

But it was a sunny fifty-two degrees this morning and he and Rachel were off to Houston with a stop along the way to visit a man he'd be happy to see dead.

He'd been up since dawn working his own ranch. He could have used a few more hours of sleep, but other than that, he had no complaints. In fact, he wasn't sure when he'd been happier.

Esther opened the door and invited him in. "Glad to see you're still kicking," she said.

"I spent years in the marines. A day of hard work isn't going to slow me down."

"Good, because you were definitely christened into the life of a Texas rancher yesterday. Pierce couldn't brag enough about you last night."

"All I heard was Pierce's crowing about his new son."

"Charlie. They named him Charlie. I'm tickled pink. I figure my Charlie is wearing the biggest smile in heaven today."

"Pierce was smiling pretty good himself last night when I stopped by the hospital."

"He was mighty happy," Esther agreed. "And Grace looked positively angelic holding her new son in her arms. Come on back to the kitchen. I'll get you some coffee. Rachel will be out in a minute."

"Sounds good." He'd hoped she'd back off the idea of having a face-to-face visit with Roy Sales, but she'd made it clear last night it was still on.

Esther poured and then handed him a mug of black coffee. "There's cream in the fridge if you want it and sugar in that chicken cup on the counter."

"No, thanks. I like it strong and black." He took a sip. "This fits the bill perfectly."

"Rachel said you're planning to bring Alfred home soon and that you'll stay on awhile if it works out."

"That's the plan."

"That's a really nice thing to do," Esther said. "I know you and your dad have had some real differences, but he was always proud of you."

"If he was, he hid it well."

"You know, I've got something I've been saving for you a long time. Alfred told me to see that you got it when he died. I figure he came close enough to dying that you should have it. Wait here. I'll get it."

Rachel arrived before Esther got back. As always, just seeing her made his insides melt. He kissed her and felt a longing that went far deeper than mere sexual desire.

"Good morning, cowboy," she said. "Or did all that work yesterday change your mind about adopting the lifestyle?"

"I'm still in. My muscles are protesting."

The truth was he'd envied Pierce his lifestyle yesterday. Not just the ranch but his life. He'd never seen a man who fit so well in his own skin.

He and Grace were a team and so in love with each other and their growing family. They seemed to have it all. Luke could get used to a life like that.

Esther rejoined them in the kitchen. She held out a sealed letter-size envelope to Luke. "I can't say if this is good or bad, but Alfred wanted you to have it. I'm just making the delivery a little soon."

He took the envelope but didn't open it. "How long have you had it?"

"I'm not sure. A year or two after you left home."

In that case, there was no reason to stop everything and read it now. He had more important things on his mind, like being with Rachel when she paid a visit to her recent and frightening past.

It wasn't how he'd have chosen to spend the day,

but Rachel thought it was necessary and who was he to argue that she was wrong?

The important thing was moving on. She deserved to feel safe and live her life to the fullest—which wouldn't necessarily include him.

DR. KINCAID ARRIVED at work early to check on his patients, especially Roy Sales. Sales had become so aggressive yesterday after hearing that Rachel Maxwell wasn't coming that the staff had to sedate him.

Kincaid wanted plenty of time to prepare him for her visit today. The longer he worked with Roy, the more uncertain he became of his true mental and emotional condition. There were days he was convinced that Sales would never be fit to face a trial.

Other days, he was certain that Roy Sales knew what he was doing and that he was running the show exactly as he planned.

Hopefully, watching him interact with the victim he continuously talked about in sessions would give Kincaid some much-needed insight.

Kincaid's office phone rang just as he was leaving to head toward Sales's floor.

"Dr. Kincaid. I'm so glad you're in early."

He could hear the alarm in the director's voice. "What's wrong?"

"One of your patients was missing at the early

morning medicine round. We're checking every nook and cranny, but he hasn't been located."

"Which patient?" Kincaid held his breath as he waited for the answer, though he was certain he already knew who it would be.

"Roy Sales. It would be impossible for him to get past the guard for his floor even if he got past the first two checkpoints. We've never had a patient escape from this facility."

"Did the night nurse report any problems?"

"No. According to the charts, his last bed check was at three fifteen. He was present and accounted for."

"I'm on my way." He prayed they wouldn't find that Sales had committed suicide—or worse.

He didn't even want to go there in his mind. He did know that if Roy Sales wasn't found soon, Rachel Maxwell would have to be warned.

LUKE AND RACHEL were about an hour away from the facility where Sales was being held when Rachel got a phone call from Sydney.

They'd talked on the phone yesterday, but those conversations had centered on Grace's giving birth. It was an exciting time and Rachel had felt as if she was right in the middle of the beautiful miracle.

"Hello, Sydney."

Sydney skipped the greeting. "Where are you?"

"On my way to Houston."

"Is Luke with you?"

"Yes, he's driving. We're in his truck."

"Good. Put the phone on Speaker. He needs to hear this, too."

She did. "What's wrong?"

"Are you still planning to stop and see Roy Sales?"

"Yes, but we're still at least an hour away."

"You have a change of plans. Don't go anywhere near that place."

"What's happened?" Luke asked, his voice tense.

"Roy Sales is missing."

"Missing. Are you saying he's escaped?" Luke asked.

"All they're saying at this point is that he's unaccounted for. He could well be still inside the facility. It's maximum security. No one has ever escaped from there before."

Rachel's heart began to pound against the walls of her chest. Her chest constricted painfully. She couldn't breathe. An all-too-familiar anxiety attack was setting in. Only this time with good reason.

"I hate to have to tell you this," Sydney said, "but you need to know. I don't think it's a good idea to go to your apartment."

"My apartment." She barely had the breath to get two words from her mouth.

"I think you should turn around and go back to Winding Creek."

"I can't go back to Winding Creek and put everyone there in danger."

"I'll take care of Rachel," Luke said, answering for her as she tried to catch her breath. "I'll be with her every second. Count on it."

"No. You don't know what you're up against," Rachel said.

"I'm a marine. I've been up against the worst that can come at you. And I'm armed with a license to carry."

"Be careful," Sydney warned. "Like I said, it's doubtful he's truly escaped, but we can't be sure of that. I'll get you updated information as soon as I hear."

"I'm counting on that," Luke said.

"Take care of my sister."

"I'll guard her with my life."

"I love you, Rachel," Sydney said. Rachel was shaking so hard she couldn't respond.

Luke pulled the car into a crowded truck stop parking area. He killed the motor and reached across the seat and took her hand. "It's okay, baby. I've got your back. I'll be right here. You're safe. I promise you, I'll keep you safe."

Her breathing slowly returned to normal. It took

moments longer for the shaking to stop and her pulse to approach normal.

"He's coming for me," she whispered, her voice shaky. "Deep in my heart, I always knew this wasn't over. It won't be over until one of us is dead."

"If anyone ends up dead, it won't be you.

"Do you still want to go to your apartment?"

"It's where I live. Just drop me off there and you can go. It's dangerous to be around me."

"Cut that crazy talk out now. I'm not going anywhere without you. We can get your things and then you're going home with me. That's settled."

"You should run like the wind to get as far away from me as you can."

"It's too late for that, sweetheart. I'm in this for as long as you'll have me."

He kissed away any further protests.

But this time he couldn't kiss the fear away.

LUKE STARED AT the endless line of unmoving cars in front of him. "Is I-10 always a parking lot?"

"During high traffic times for the commuters, but not at this time of the day. There must be a wreck ahead."

"In every lane?"

"They usually try to keep a lane or two open for rubberneckers."

Luke knew she was trying hard not to succumb to

the memories and resurfacing fears. As strong-willed as she was, he hated to think what her captivity had been like for it to have such a powerful effect on her.

"Traffic is a mess, but then, millions of people call the Houston metropolis home."

"I'll never be one of them."

The stupidity of that remark was obvious the second the words cleared his mouth. This was her home and he had no right to knock it.

"I'm sure Houston has a lot to offer. Professional football, baseball, basketball and the largest indoor rodeo in the country, or so I've heard."

"It also has theater, a great symphony and world-class museums. The sad part is I spent so much time working I seldom took advantage of any of it. Fitch, Fitch and Bauman was my life."

"Did the firm require it?"

"When I first started, wrapping up billable hours was the measuring by which the newly hired were judged. But even after that, I had a humongous need to outwork everyone else. I demanded far too much of myself."

"That sounds like a sure path to burnout."

"I was probably headed for that. I was reminded yesterday of how isolated I'd become from friends and family and from the drama of day-to-day life. The truth is I can't remember not being driven."

"Maybe you need someone around to remind

you to smell the roses or kick the ball—something like that."

She smiled. "Or someone to soak me with the water hose every now and then?"

"Or treat you to room service."

"That will work equally well. Thanks for helping me through the anxiety attack. Hearing that Sales has possibly escaped sucked me right back into the trauma. I'm still partially there."

"That's not a sign of weakness. It's a sign you're normal."

The traffic began to inch forward. A half mile farther and they reached the cause of the delay. Two cop cars, one tow truck loaded with a severely damaged compact car and one pickup on the shoulder that had survived the incident with barely a dent.

"The good news is we're practically at my apartment," Rachel said. "Take the next exit and then turn right at the light."

Rachel was silent the rest of the way except for giving directions. His mind went back to Sales. Luke had hoped to hear from Sydney by now that he'd been found and returned to his supposedly secure area.

They made a couple more turns before Rachel had him pull into a large parking garage. She pushed her remote, and the doors opened.

They took the elevator to her floor. One look inside the apartment and he was beyond impressed. "I feel like I'm taking a tour of the rich and famous. Did you inherit your fortune or do attorneys actually get paid this well?"

"No inheritance, and it's not as expensive as it looks. It's also safe and extremely convenient. That means a lot when you work in the city."

The place was spotlessly clean, not a throw pillow, a cushion or a knickknack out of order. The room smelled of vanilla, likely from the scented candles in stunning containers placed about the room.

"It's hard to believe that the woman who lives here was actually scrubbing my kitchen three nights ago."

"Sydney always says I got the family neat-freak gene." Rachel kicked off her shoes. "Make yourself at home. There's wine in the bar just off the kitchen and whiskey and some vodka, I think. No beer. Sorry about that."

"Whiskey always works. What can I get you?"

"Nothing yet."

Luke decided to check out the bedroom first. It didn't look like a place to kick off cowboy boots, but it did have a king-size bed.

Unless they got good news from Sydney, this would not be the night to try it out appropriately, but at least he could sleep beside her and hold her in his arms.

For all the lavish amenities, he'd rather be back at Arrowhead Hills. But only if Rachel was there with him. He had no intention of letting her out of his sight until Roy Sales was found and locked away again.

RACHEL JUMPED WHEN her phone rang, and then dashed across the living room to retrieve it. Her heart sank when she saw the caller was Claire Covey.

"Hayden's here," Claire said. "He's home." Her voice rang with joy. "I know you mentioned a possible meeting on Wednesday. We can meet you anytime today."

"I know what I said, but unfortunately this isn't a good day for me."

"I'm begging you to meet with us if only for a few minutes. I can meet you anywhere in Houston and any time you say. I'll just feel so much better about everything once you get to talk to Hayden one-on-one."

Claire was clearly overcome with optimism and the excitement of having her son out of jail. It was difficult to put her off.

"He knows things the police aren't saying." Claire insisted.

"What kind of things?"

"That information will be better coming from him. He's innocent. After you talk to him you'll realize that. Please. He's so scared. He needs to know someone besides his father and me are on his side."

"You do understand that this will only be an interview," Rachel said. "I can't make a commitment this soon for a variety of reasons."

"He didn't kill Louann Black. What other reasons could possibly matter?"

"I have to trust him to level with me. This isn't a game. I can't accept lies or omissions from him. And he may not feel comfortable working with me."

"He'll tell the truth. He has nothing to hide."

It could be that Hayden Covey was as innocent as his mother claimed. Or he could be a brutal killer who deserved to pay for his crime.

Rachel still couldn't rule out the chance that the evil she had sensed in him might have been only a reflection of the way she felt about Roy Sales. "Okay, I'm in downtown Houston," Rachel said, giving in to Claire's pleas. "I can see him now if that works for you."

"We can be there in thirty minutes. Just give me an address."

Rachel gave her the directions.

Take two on Hayden Covey. Innocent or a psycho.

Hopefully Rachel would make the right call.

Chapter Seventeen

Rachel sat across from Hayden Covey in the small office connected to her dining area. Luke and Claire were on the balcony that overlooked the pool, ensuring Rachel and Hayden absolute privacy.

Claire hadn't wanted it that way. Rachel had insisted.

Rachel didn't feel the immediate evil vibes she had sensed on Friday. They would be starting fresh. "Tell me about yourself, Hayden."

"I thought this was supposed to be about the way the police are trying to railroad me just because they don't like my dad."

"We'll get to that later. First I'd just like to get to know you better."

"I'm a running back for University of Texas. I was mentioned for the Heisman this year. I didn't get nominated, but some people think if I stay on the top of my game next year, I'll be a shoo-in."

"Obviously football is very important to you."

"Yeah, well, I like it, and I'm good at it."

"What else are you good at?"

"Most every type of sports. Dad says I'm a born athlete. I'm disciplined. Never miss a practice, hardly ever miss a game. I play hurt."

"What are your interests besides sports?"

"Mostly just hanging out with the guys on the team."

"What do you do when you hang out?"

"You know. Guy stuff."

"Do you date much?"

"Some."

"Tell me about Louann Black."

He started to squirm. "It's nothing like the police are saying, I can promise you that."

"What's it like?"

"We dated for a few months. We had some good times. It was never anything serious."

"Did Louann want it to be serious?"

"No. She was a party girl. Drank too much. Always wanting me to buy drugs for her. It got old."

"But you didn't break up with her?"

"I was getting around to it. She heard about it and dumped me first. No big deal."

Not until Louann was murdered.

"You must have been shocked to hear that she'd been killed."

"I was, but I was nowhere around her the night it

happened. I hadn't seen her for days. I've got people who'll swear to that."

He had people, but he also had money, and people could be bought.

Their interview lasted for two hours, in which time Hayden changed the story about his relationship with Louann at least three times. That was never a good sign, but sometimes defendants just said what they thought you wanted to hear, especially when they were scared.

Hayden was clearly scared. Rachel wasn't convinced he was innocent, but it was early in the process. She had a lot of research to do on him, Louann and the police report before she could make a studied decision.

She had a good detective friend in Homicide who might shed a bit more light on the subject. As soon as Claire and Hayden left, she'd give Matt a call.

Right now she just wanted to get the news that Roy Sales was back in his supposedly secure facility.

It was ten minutes before ten and Rachel had already showered and slipped into a pale blue satin nightshirt when Sydney finally called.

Rachel answered on the first ring and pressed Speaker so Luke could hear what was said. "Tell me you're calling with good news."

"I'd love to, but the facility administrator is still

trying to sell the idea that Sales is hiding out somewhere inside the building. He's convinced Sales couldn't breach every safeguard they have in place."

"Only because he doesn't know Roy Sales the way I do."

"I'm starting to have my doubts, as well. I wish they'd call in the FBI so I could be official instead of relying on back channels—legally, of course. Did you decide to spend the night in Houston?"

"Yes. Luke and I are in my apartment. I haven't made any decisions about what I'll do tomorrow but we're definitely staying here tonight."

"I don't think you should be anyplace alone until Sales is located."

"I'm not going anywhere without her," Luke promised.

"So don't worry about me," Rachel said to assure her sister. "I'm protected by a genuine hero-status former member of the US Marines."

"That does ease my mind a bit. I'll give you a call in the morning or before if I hear something. You do the same."

"I will. I just keep wondering if my not showing up to see Sales yesterday instigated any of this."

"Don't go getting the idea that any of this is your fault."

"It was just a thought." A very disturbing thought that she was having trouble shaking.

Rachel was still pondering that possibility long after the call from Sydney was finished. She walked over and sat on the bed beside Luke. She couldn't miss seeing the weapon on the table beside the bed.

"You look worried." He slipped an arm around her waist. "Are you afraid that I might not be a match for Roy Sales?"

She thought about it before she answered, "The memories are so sickening that they pull me back into the fear without warning. But no. I'm never afraid when I'm with you."

"In that case, let's get some sleep. After the way this week has started, there's no telling what tomorrow will bring. Besides, this will be our first night to sleep together."

He pulled down the top sheet and crawled into bed.

Rachel hesitated. "I feel safe with you, but I'm not sure I can re-create the magic of Monday's afternoon delight. I couldn't do the night or us justice."

"I'm not expecting you to."

She crawled in beside him. He rolled over to face her and trailed a finger along her lips. "We never talked about it," he said, "and we don't have to talk about it now, but when I picture that monster touching you, abusing you, defiling you, the rage roars inside me."

"He defiled me in many ways, but not sexually," she said, understanding what he was thinking even if he couldn't bring himself to say the words. "He touched me inappropriately a few times, but only on my breasts and thighs.

"It was never about sex with him, though he threatened it. It was all about control and pleasing his dead mother, who'd once abused him. That seemed to be the root of his madness, but his evil seemed to come from hell itself."

"I'd love to come face-to-face with the slimy bastard. I'd wring his neck with my bare hands."

They snuggled together, his chest to her back, his muscular thigh sliding in between her legs, his breath falling on the nape of her neck.

Her world was falling apart, and yet it never seemed more together than when she was in Luke Dawkins's arms.

RACHEL WOKE TO the first light of day sliding through her blinds. She'd slept so soundly it took a moment to realize where she was. She rolled over, reached out for Luke and felt a wave of disappointment that he wasn't there.

She went to the bathroom and splashed her face with cold water. In spite of not knowing Sale's whereabouts, it was the best night's sleep she'd had since the abduction.

She found Luke in the kitchen, staring at the blinking light on her one-server coffee maker.

"I was going to brew coffee and bring you a cup in bed, but the blinking blue light refuses to let me."

"Here, let me do it."

A minute later she handed him his cup.

"I'd cook breakfast, but your fridge is empty except for butter, ketchup and a few other condiments. Your pantry isn't much better."

"I don't do a lot of cooking. I usually pick up a bagel on the way to work, and that holds me until lunch."

"Don't let Esther hear you say that. She'll force-feed you bacon until you oink."

"If I could cook as well as Esther, I'd change my eating habits."

"What is our plan for today?" Luke asked.

"I know you need to get back to the ranch and perhaps check on Alfred."

"I can spare another day if you have things to take care of here—like talking to Eric Fitch Sr. or seeing Hayden Covey again."

"I need to find out more details of Louann Black's murder before I see Hayden or his mother. And I need to decide what I'm going to do about that before I discuss a future with the firm."

"Have you considered other options for a career?"

"A few."

Her phone rang and she raced back to the bedroom to get it.

It was Dr. Kincaid. She whispered a prayer that this was good news.

Chapter Eighteen

"Good morning, Dr. Kincaid."

"Is this Rachel Maxwell?"

"Yes, and I do hope you have some good news."

"I wish that were the case. Unfortunately, I fear just the opposite."

"Then Roy Sales has escaped the facility?"

"We don't have positive proof of that, but the buildings and grounds have been thoroughly searched and there's no sign of him."

"I was afraid of that from the beginning. I appreciate you giving me the heads-up."

"There's another reason I called. I don't know what the law authorities are going to tell you, but I've worked with Sales for months now. He's obsessed with you and convinced you betrayed him."

"That is a really warped way of looking at things after what he put me through."

"In my judgment, he's a really sick man. I have a strong suspicion that he's going to try to kill you.

Whether it's to satisfy him or his mother, I can't be sure. But I do think your life is at risk until he's found and taken back into custody."

"Have you told anyone else this?"

"I've told the administration and I just talked to your sister, Sydney. I'm sure she'll have advice for keeping you safe. Follow it."

"I will. I do have one question. Do you think my not showing up to visit him as planned triggered this?"

"It may have had something to do with the timing, but he didn't just conceive of an escape plan one day and execute it the next. Not from this facility. This had to be something he was working on for months, probably ever since he's been here."

"Thanks again for calling," she said, "but I have to go. I have another call coming through now. I'm sure it's Sydney."

"Good. If you have any other questions, feel free to call me."

"I will." She went straight to Sydney's call.

Sydney repeated what she'd heard from Dr. Kincaid before switching to her own take on everything.

"Don't panic," Sydney cautioned. "I'm sure every law enforcement officer in the state—from local to the Texas Rangers—is looking for the Lone Star Snatcher."

"What do you suggest I do?"

"Hire a bodyguard. I'll fax you a list of reliable sources in your area. Enlist them for 24/7 service and then follow their orders. Or just let me know where you'll be and I can take care of everything."

"I have a bodyguard."

"Doesn't he have a ranch to run and a father to take care of?"

"He does." Expecting more from him was unreasonable. "Send me the list. I'll hire bodyguard protection."

She was just starting to get a grip on life again. She would not let Sales snatch that away.

"I DON'T LIKE IT," Luke said. "I respect your sister's judgment, but this time I think she's wrong."

"You don't have to stay here with me, Luke. Drive back to the ranch. I can find a way to get my car from Esther's house later."

"What is it you don't understand about I'm not leaving here without you. Besides, going back to Winding Creek and staying with me makes a lot more sense."

"You have a ranch to run."

"To hell with the ranch."

"You don't mean that, and I can't let you spend your every second looking out for me."

"If you don't go back to Winding Creek with

me, then I'm not going back, so you're not doing me any favors."

"Did you get your stubbornness from Alfred?"

"Insults won't change my mind."

And the truth was she didn't want to change his mind. She wanted to go back to Arrowhead Hills. She wanted to sleep in Luke's arms every night and have coffee with him every morning. She might even learn to make pancakes or fry eggs.

"I'll go back with you to Winding Creek under one condition."

"Name it," Luke said.

"I hire a protection service not only for me but for Esther's ranch, as well."

"Does Roy Sales know Esther?"

"He killed her husband."

"Point made."

"If you want bodyguards, we'll have bodyguards, but you'll be at Arrowhead Hills, not in Houston."

"You've got yourself a deal."

She had only one stop to make before they left Houston.

THE POLICE PRECINCT was hopping, but Matt managed to find a few minutes for Rachel. They were usually working for opposites sides and purposes, but they had a mutual respect for each other.

As far as Rachel was concerned, he was the best

homicide detective in the city. She'd have loved to include Luke in their discussion but was afraid Matt would hold something back with him in the room.

Matt wouldn't give her any information that hadn't already been released to the public, but she'd pick up a lot from how he said it.

Matt grabbed an armload of files off a metal folding chair and piled them on his already cluttered desk.

"Have a seat."

She did.

He propped his backside on the corner of his desk. "I'd like to say 'Good to see you,' but 'Are you nuts?' has a more appropriate ring to it."

"Any particular reason?"

"It's all over the news that you're defending a murdering piece of... You get the picture."

"I take it you're convinced Hayden is guilty."

"Without a doubt. Have you seen the police report?"

"Not yet. I'm not officially on the case yet in spite of what you hear on the news."

"Then I take it you haven't seen the crime scene pictures, either?"

"No."

"They're as brutal as I've ever seen. Lots of slashing. Enough blood to fill a barrel."

"Hayden claims he's innocent," Rachel said.

"He isn't. We've got enough evidence to bury him,

and he knows it. He's counting on his parents to save him. And now I guess he's counting on you, too."

"I haven't seen a lot of motive for murder, as yet," Rachel said. "There's lots of hearsay but nothing solid."

"Believe me, you'll hear it at the trial. He's guilty. But he's smart, hard to trip up when you're talking to him. You think you've seen evil? You've never seen it the way you're gonna face it in Hayden Covey. He's guilty and he's going down. Represent him, and you will, too."

"I'll keep that in mind."

"By the way, I heard about Roy Sales breaking out of the psychiatric hospital, or at least disappearing. That's another one who should have gone directly to death row. Not worth the air he's breathing."

"I couldn't agree more."

"He won't stay on the loose long. Every cop in the state is dying to arrest the Lone Star Snatcher."

"That's what I hear," Rachel said.

"In the meantime, stay safe. I can't imagine him wanting to get anywhere near you and your FBI sister, but you never can tell what a lunatic will do."

"I'll be careful. And thanks."

"Yeah. Take what I told you about Hayden as gospel. I'm not bluffing. I'm dead serious this time."

She stood and he walked her to the door, picking up a file and handing it to her as she left.

"A little bedtime entertainment—if you're looking for nightmares. By the way, you didn't get this from me, even though it's not confidential since it's already been leaked. It's just too brutal for the media to show. It's already making the rounds on the internet, though."

Fortunately, Rachel didn't wait until bedtime to open the file. She didn't even wait for Luke to back out of his parking space.

She took one look at the gory crime scene shot inside the file and gagged, struggling not to throw up.

Luke killed the engine. "What's wrong?"

She handed him the picture.

He didn't hold back the curses that expressed his feelings. She would have been shocked if he did.

"If there's a chance Hayden Covey is guilty of that, I don't want you around him unless I'm there with you." Hayden Covey might be innocent, but whoever murdered Louann Black needed to be convicted. That kind of evil wasn't just bone deep. It went to the deepest pits of the soul. Roy Sales had taught her that.

If she had any doubts of Hayden's innocence, she would never be able to defend him.

Rachel took out her phone and made a call to Claire Covey. "Some things have come up and I need to see your son as soon as possible."

"He's not here right now. He's with friends and

I'm not sure when he'll be back. Will tomorrow afternoon work?"

"I'll be back in Winding Creek by then."

"I can get him there. Where shall we meet you?"

"I'd like to see him by himself this time."

"Fine. I'll get a hotel room and we'll stay in Winding Creek as long as you need us. I can't rest until I know you're on our side."

"Then I'll see you tomorrow at two."

Rachel gave her directions to the ranch. She was leaning strongly toward turning down the case, but she'd give Hayden one more chance to convince her he was innocent.

She studied the picture again and then tossed it into the back seat.

LUKE AND PIERCE took their mugs of hot coffee and a couple of Esther's famous oatmeal cookies to Pierce's front porch. Rachel, last seen cradling baby Charlie in her arms and crooning baby talk to him, had stayed inside with Esther and Grace.

"There have been some new developments with Roy Sales," Luke said. "He's missing from the maximum-security facility where he was being held."

"I heard about it from Sheriff Cavazos and from Sydney and Tucker. It's also being reported all over the internet. I'm sure it will make the evening news. Can't keep something like that quiet."

"They managed to keep it quiet for a day," Luke said. "I guess you also know that Sydney has handled the hiring of protection services for both our ranches."

"Sydney called and told me she's hired protection for the ranch and that will include my house and Esther's and bodyguards for Esther and Grace. I told her it was a waste of money. I have the manpower to protect my own ranch. Every one of us can drop the hammer and hit the target faster than you can sneeze."

"What did she say?" Luke asked.

"She had Tucker call me. He convinced me it would be much easier to give in to Sydney and Rachel on this than to argue with them. Hopefully we're talking about only a few days before they recapture Sales."

"Is Esther going along with this?"

"Surprisingly, yes. She's staying with us a few days anyway to help Grace out with Charlie. She thinks it will be a hoot to have a bodyguard help her feed the chickens and gather eggs."

"We need a video of that. Is Grace okay with having a personal bodyguard?"

"She says I'm all the bodyguard she needs, but she's willing to put up with it. I think she's secretly glad to have it. She's faced enough terror in her own life. And Jaci is staying with Riley and Dani a few days so she won't be frightened by strangers with guns hanging around the house."

"When are you expecting your strangers with guns?" Luke asked.

"Five o'clock."

"Same here."

"There's plenty of room for Rachel at our place if she wants to stay here," Pierce offered.

"She's staying with me," Luke assured him.

"I kind of figured that. It's fine with me, by the way. I know she's in good hands."

IT WAS FOUR O'CLOCK when Rachel and Luke finished putting away the groceries they'd bought at the local grocery. The pantry was officially full. So was the refrigerator.

Luke knew it wasn't official or lasting, but it felt as if he and Rachel were setting up house together. He liked the feeling. He'd like it even better with her sleeping in his bed tonight.

Rachel stood at the open door of the refrigerator, staring at the full shelves. "Do you like beef stew?"

"Doesn't everybody?"

"I think I'll call Esther and ask her for her recipe. I'm sure hers will be delicious. And how hard can stew be?"

"You don't have to go to that much trouble. I can grill some steaks."

"I think we need stew. It's comfort food, and after the last few days, I could use a lot of comfort."

He started to remind her they had an hour before the cavalry arrived and that time could be better spent. He figured that might be pushing things. He didn't want her to think this was all about sex for him, especially with all she was dealing with.

Luke grabbed a cold beer and his jacket and walked out to the porch while Rachel got started on her stew project.

The letter Esther had given him was folded and in the back pocket of his jeans. He pulled it out, looked at the envelope for a few minutes and finally broke the seal.

He settled on the top porch step and finished his beer before he started to read.

Son,
If you're reading this, I'm dead, but there's things I need to say. I'm not the man I wanted to be. Not the man I needed to be. If I were, things might have turned out differently for all of us.

I'm not blaming this on anyone, but I was raised by Grandpa Hank. You never met him, but he was one of the meanest scoundrels in the county. I tried hard not to be like him. I didn't do so good at that.

I never showed it right, but I loved your mother more than anything in the world. I love you, too. I never said it, but I'm proud of you.

All I got to leave you is Arrowhead Hills Ranch. I own it free and clear. If you don't want it, sell it and take the money. You deserve the life you want. Would like it if you make sure the horses get good homes when you sell them.

My will is in my safe-deposit box up at the bank on Main Street with everything else that's worth saving.

I got lots of regrets and I'm not even dying yet. I figure when I do, won't nobody shed a tear. Can't blame them. Don't be a fool like me. Find a woman you can love and show her how much every day of your life.

Alfred P. Dawkins.

PS, I should have come and watched you play ball that day.

Luke blinked hard to hold back the tears as he folded the letter and slipped it back in his pocket.

It didn't change everything, but it was the best look he'd ever gotten into his dad's mind. The first time Alfred had ever told him he loved him or was proud of him.

THIS PART OF the parking lot at a small neighborhood grocery store was nearly empty as the elderly woman opened the back seat of her car and deposited her handbag and a shopping bag.

Roy waited until she was settling behind the wheel before he approached her car from behind. She closed her door and started the engine. He jumped from behind her car and dived into the back seat where she'd put the packages.

"What do you want?" Her voice trembled.

"A ride."

"Who are you?"

"Your worst nightmare." Roy pulled the sharp carving knife from his boot holster and flashed it for her to see.

She screamed.

He fit his hand around the back of her neck. "Shut up now or I'll cut out your tongue. Do exactly as I say and you won't get hurt. Leave the engine running and get out of the car. Call the cops and I'll come back and kill you."

He took his hands from the woman's neck. She jumped from the car, started to run, then slipped and fell. The back of her head hit the concrete, and blood splattered everywhere.

Roy gunned the engine and sped away. He'd hide out until it was full dark and then he'd take the back roads to Winding Creek. He'd wasted too much time already, only to learn that she'd quit her job. No luck at her apartment, either. No sign of movement and no lights had come on at dark.

He wouldn't take the risk of getting past the apartment's security only to break into an empty apartment.

He figured his next best hope of finding her was at the Double K Ranch. Esther Kavanaugh wouldn't have hesitated to take her in. Hopefully he'd find Rachel and Esther alone in the sprawling ranch house.

Roy loved the way the news kept saying he couldn't possibly have escaped the infamous barred asylum. They'd underestimated him. Everyone always did.

He laid the knife on the seat beside him and ran his index finger along the razor-sharp edge. The crazy thing was he hadn't even had to use it to escape. The meanest guard in the place had worked it all out for him.

The guard had sent him through the gates in the back of a truck carrying medical waste that no one ever wanted to look in or to touch.

Roy wasn't afraid. He was in his own bag with only a few air holes to let him breathe.

It was all in the way you played the game.

All Roy had had to do was promise to kill someone for the hated guard. He might even keep the promise.

But first he'd take care of Rachel Maxwell. People who betrayed you must pay.

Mommy would be proud of him.

Chapter Nineteen

Luke took one bite of the stew, and his tongue caught fire. He forced himself to swallow. "Wow!"

"Do you like it?"

"Love it. It's a little spicy and maybe a tad too much salt, but that's the way I love it."

Rachel dipped her spoon into her bowl and took a bite. She didn't swallow, but ran to the sink to spit it out. "It's horrible. How could you say you loved it?"

"I'm tactful?"

"I followed the recipe except that Esther doesn't have real measurements. She says pinch of this, tad of that, a handful of this, a dozen peppers."

"A dozen peppers. What kind of peppers?"

"Jalapeños."

"She told you to use a dozen jalapeños?"

"Yes, but I didn't have that many, so I added the two jars of sliced ones we bought at the store."

"That explains the fire."

Rachel checked the recipe. "Oops. There is a tiny

little hyphen between the one and the two. Don't know how I missed that. I thought twelve sounded like a lot."

"I'm sure if you hadn't misread the recipe the stew would have been delicious."

"I guess I'd best not offer any to the hired protection."

"Not if you want them to save you. Tell you what, I'll make us a BLT sandwich. The guys seem to have all they need except a bathroom in that fancy van of theirs."

"They assured me they didn't need a thing," Rachel said. "But a BLT sounds good to me. I actually can fry bacon and I'm a whiz at slicing tomatoes."

"But how are you at toasting bread?"

"You're just plain making fun of me now."

He walked over, wrapped his arms around her waist and nibbled on her earlobe. "I would never do that. So how about you start frying and slicing and I'll go lay a fire in the fireplace? Might as well add a romantic touch to our gourmet meal."

"You do realize there will be a shortage of privacy," Rachel said. "You never know when one of the guards will need a bathroom break."

"Yes, but I have something I want to talk to you about and it's still a little muddy to take a walk in your cute little suede booties. You'll have to get a pair of real cowboy boots if you're going to make it on the ranch."

A stupid comment. He'd had to practically force her to come home with him this time and she was in danger. He'd had no indication from her she was interested in leaving her lush Houston apartment for the boondocks.

"You sound serious," Rachel said. "Is this about Roy Sales?"

"No."

"Then start the fire."

RACHEL'S JAW CLENCHED as she started frying the bacon. Her stomach churned. It was her typical first reaction at anything to do with a fire.

She was with Luke. She could do this.

By the time they were cuddled in front of the fire and munching on their sandwiches, her impulsive fears had dissolved. Luke kept the talk pleasant with no mention of Roy or the security personnel standing guard over the house and immediate surrounding area.

When they'd finished eating, he walked over and stoked the fire. Before sitting down, he took a folded letter from his back pocket and handed it to her. "Esther gave me this Tuesday. She was supposed to give it to me when Alfred died, though I'm not sure why he was so confident she'd outlive him or exactly why she decided to give it to me now, but she did."

"It must be personal," Rachel said. "Are you sure you want me to read it?"

"I'm sure."

She unfolded the letter and started to read. Tears filled her eyes before she reached the end.

"He told you a lot in a few words," Rachel said. "A lifetime of regrets."

"So it seems."

"The two of you must have always had a strained relationship."

Luke sat back down beside her. "We never really had a relationship of any kind. I don't remember having one meaningful conversation with him. Nothing except complaints about whatever I tried to do. I finally started doing things that angered him on purpose."

"Your mother must have felt the same heartbreak you did."

"I blamed Alfred for her death. He drove her away. She died before the two of us could have a life that offered more than endless putdowns."

"And yet he sounds sincere when he says he loved you both. That must touch you."

"It does. I'm not sure what our chances are of ever having anything that approaches a father/son relationship, but maybe there's a chance for us to live together in some sort of harmony. At least I'm willing to try."

She squeezed his hand as a tear rolled down her cheek. "What game was he talking about that he missed? It has clearly lain heavy on his mind for all these years."

"My high school baseball team was playing in the state championship. I was to be the pitcher and several major league scouts were going to be there to watch me pitch. It was the biggest day in my life to that point, one that could have affected the rest of my life."

"Why didn't he go?"

"He was doing the spring roundup and branding that day. The plans were made before we knew we were going to state. He'd hired the extras he needed. When I told him I wouldn't be around to help, he exploded. The ranch was everything to him and he thought it should be to me, too. He told me if I went to the game, I didn't need to come home."

"And you didn't?"

"I didn't."

"What about your chance to play professional baseball?"

"I blew it. I didn't even graduate, just drove up to Austin after the game and joined the marines.

"It was a long time before I even admitted to myself that I wasn't only furious. Finally admitting to myself that he cared nothing about me and would rather I be out of his life devastated me."

"Of course it did. You were only eighteen. That game was the biggest thing in your life."

"Crazy thing is, now that I'm back here on the ranch, I realize I never hated ranching. It's likely in my blood as much as it is in his. I was just tired of life the way it was."

"So much hurt," Rachel said. "So much misunderstanding. So many years lost."

Luke put an arm around her shoulder and pulled her close.

At least Luke knew what he wanted to do with his life now. She didn't, but she was having serious doubts about ever going back to criminal defense.

It was a worthy profession. It saved many innocent people from being punished for crimes they didn't commit. It forced the courts to present solid evidence and then hope for the jury to make sound decisions.

Sometimes they failed. Most of the time they didn't.

It just wasn't the life for her, at least not now. Maybe it never would be, but she had plenty of time to make up her mind.

She couldn't wait where Hayden Covey was concerned. It wasn't fair to him or his parents. Right or wrong, she was not convinced of his innocence.

Eric Fitch Sr. would represent him far better than she could.

She'd call Claire Covey tonight.

Now all she had to worry about was a madman who wanted her dead.

RACHEL'S PHONE RANG in the wee hours of the morning, waking her from a sound sleep. She sat up in bed and grabbed her phone. "Hello."

"This is Sheriff Cavazos. I'm calling about Roy Sales."

Chapter Twenty

Rachel's heart pounded.

"What about Roy Sales?"

Luke sat up in bed beside her, his hand on her back.

"He's dead," Cavazos said.

She couldn't have heard that right. Sales didn't die. He tortured and ruined lives. He murdered. "Are you sure?"

"I pulled the trigger that sent the bullet through his brains myself."

"Sales is dead," she whispered to Luke. "I'm switching the call to Speaker so Luke can listen in," she told Cavazos.

If she'd had any hope that people in Winding Creek didn't know she was sleeping with Luke, she'd just blown that.

"How did it happen?" she asked.

"Good law enforcement. I knew you had those high-dollar guards over at Pierce's cabin, so I had deputies watching the main gate and the back gate at the Double K Ranch. I figured if Sales came to Winding Creek looking for revenge, he'd show up at Esther's spread first."

"Really?" That surprised Luke. "From what Sales's psychiatrist said, we figured his first strike would be against Rachel."

"Exactly. We think he tried her apartment first and must have found out she wasn't there."

"How do you know that?" Rachel asked.

"A man fitting Sales's description carjacked a woman in a parking lot a few blocks from your apartment. She was found bleeding from a head wound and with a concussion. Sales's style of brutality, though she says she fell as he drove away in her car.

"She still managed to ID him for the officer who showed up to investigate," Cavazos continued. "The report was all over law enforcement wires. He ditched the car about thirty miles from Winding Creek."

"So he ditched one car, picked up another and headed to Esther's place," Luke surmised.

"Yep," Cavazos said. "It was common knowledge Rachel and her sister spent some time at the Double K Ranch with Esther after Sales was first arrested."

Rachel took a deep breath and exhaled slowly. "I'm having a hard time getting my head around the fact that Roy Sales is really dead."

"I understand that after what he put you through.

But it was going to happen sooner or later," Cavazos said. "I'm just glad it happened before he hurt or killed someone else. Too much evil stewing around in his sick mind."

"I don't see how anyone could argue with that," Luke said.

"I s'pect you'd have enjoyed dropping the hammer on him yourself, Luke. Probably better I beat you to it. Less paperwork and headaches for you."

"No doubt," Luke agreed.

"I'm heading over to Pierce's house now," Cavazos said. "I figure I'd best let them all know what took place at their back gate this morning. I could use some hot coffee, and one of Esther's breakfasts would taste mighty good this morning, too. It's been a long night."

"I'm sure you'll get breakfast," Rachel said, "along with many thanks. I'm still practically speechless, so I know I'm not doing an adequate job of thanking you myself."

"That goes for me, as well," Luke said. "I plan to be moving to Winding Creek permanently. If there's ever anything I can help you with, all it takes is a call."

"Careful what you offer," Cavazos said. "Never know when I might need to deputize a former medaled marine. Even a small, friendly town like Winding Creek gets hit by trouble every now and then."

"A little too often for me," Rachel said.

"Yes, but you can let those high-priced gun-toting gorillas off your dime. You've got nothing to worry about now. We'll talk more soon."

Cavazos made it sound like a done deal. She knew the trauma of her time in captivity wouldn't disappear in an instant. But for the first time she was confident that she'd move past it.

She cuddled back in Luke's arms. But not to sleep.

They made love until the sun shot its first golden rays over the horizon. Time enough to release the bodyguards that she hoped never to need again.

HAYDEN COVEY WAS watching from a well-hidden spot when he saw a white van carrying two men drive down the hard dirt ranch road and approach the Arrowhead Hills Ranch gate. The passenger who got out to unlatch the gate did not look like your typical Texas cowboy.

He was missing the familiar Western hat but was wearing a pair of stylish aviator sunglasses. He wore a black long-sleeved T-shirt over jeans that looked like they'd never seen a horse or even a lot of wear, for that matter. A large semiautomatic pistol was holstered at his waist.

Looked like a security guard to Hayden.

The lawyer babe must really be running scared if she was hiring protection. Guess her own cowboy, the guy called Luke something or other, wasn't tough enough to keep her safe from the crazy guy who was after her.

Not that it mattered to Hayden. He wouldn't be dealing with Luke. He liked things one-on-one with the odds always in his favor. He'd teach that bitch to give him the runaround and then turn against him.

He was getting enough crap from the homicide detectives. He wasn't about to take it from her. Besides, he'd never even be suspected of killing her. She already had a genuine nutcase killer after her.

He put his earphones back in his ears and let the banging background bass get him even more stirred up. He'd been driving most of the night. He needed to stay awake a few more hours.

He drove to the gate, got out and swung it open before getting back into a stolen car and barreling over the cattle gap.

A stolen car that would never be traced back to Hayden.

Chapter Twenty-One

Rachel pulled the sheets from the bed in Alfred's room. The thin drapes needed laundering, as well. Better yet, they should be trashed. She'd see what kind of replacement she could find in town or online.

In her mind, the best homecoming for Alfred would be a house that was spotlessly clean from floor to ceiling. Luke had his own ideas about what Alfred needed on the functional side.

He'd just left to go talk to one of the wranglers about some special feed they needed for the quarter horses. He was driving into town then to pick up the feed and some safety support rails and grab bars to install in the bathroom and anywhere else Alfred might need them.

There was plenty of work to do, but Rachel couldn't keep from humming as she added the sheets and some detergent to the washing machine.

There was really no reason she was still here now that she was out of danger. No reason except that she was unemployed and had no reason to rush back to Houston. The main reason she was still here was Luke, not that she expected what they had going for them was permanent. He'd never mentioned forever, and things were too unsettled for either of them right now to make firm plans for the future.

The front door creaked open as she started the washer.

"Back so soon?" she called. "What did you forget?"

The footsteps grew louder. There was no answer. She walked back to the kitchen. Hayden Covey was standing there, a black briefcase in his right hand.

His clothes were rumpled, as if he'd slept in his car. He looked around as if sizing up the place.

"I wasn't expecting you this morning," she said. "Didn't your mother give you my message?"

"You mean that message where you said to hell with me, you had your own problems?"

"I'm sure you know that's not what I said. I explained everything to your mother. I know she was upset, but I thought she understood that I was not in a good place to represent you. Eric Fitch Sr. will do a much better job."

"She understood, all right. We both understand. You've already decided I'm guilty." He placed his briefcase on the kitchen table, unlatching but not opening it.

Rachel met his gaze and was instantly struck with that same aura of evil she'd first felt at the law firm. Anxiety dried her lips and made her hands clammy.

"I decided to do some explaining myself," Hayden said.

"What do you want to explain?"

"How it was with me and Louann. Louann was no innocent young coed. She liked sex and she liked it dirty. Handcuffs, whips, hot candle wax. You know what I'm talking about.?"

Cold sweat broke out on Rachel's forehead and between her breasts. Her stomach churned.

"I'm not complaining," Hayden said. "I gave her all the pain she wanted, but that wasn't good enough. She found someone else, a nice guy, she said, who treated her like a lady. She didn't want to see me anymore."

She forced a semi-calm to her voice. "That must have upset you."

"Not much. Louann wasn't that great in bed. Wasn't that pretty, either. What pissed me off was the way she started spreading all kinds of lies about me around campus. Saying I was a control freak, that I was a psycho with a temper."

"If those were lies, I can see why they made you angry." She was playing along with him now. If he kept this up, he just might confess.

"I don't need that trash talk about me. I'm the star of the football team. I'm pro football material."

Rachel eased backward, closer to the counter that held the knife block—just in case this turned really ugly. "Is that why you killed her?"

"I warned her. She didn't listen. But you should have heard how she screamed when I made that first slash with the jagged-edged hunting knife. Guess she didn't want to be gutted."

Rachel reached for the longest, sharpest knife. She yanked it from the block and pointed it at Hayden. "Get out. Get out now."

"Or you'll do what, kill me? I don't think so."

But he turned and started walking away. Her heart was in her throat. Her insides were tied into knots. Despite the fear, she knew she'd kill him if she had to, but she didn't want to.

In a split second, he turned back toward her, grabbed something from his briefcase and tackled her to the floor.

He straddled her, pinning her wrists to the floor, rendering her knife useless. She tried to force him off her, but he was incredibly strong. She screamed, praying one of the hands would be near enough to hear her.

No one came.

Hayden released one wrist. She slammed a fist into his face and then tried to jam her fingers into his eyes. She was fighting for her life. For her future. For the chance to be with Luke Dawkins.

That was when she saw the ropes dangling from Hayden's hand. The briefcase was open. Apparently he'd stored his ropes and who knew what else in there.

He slammed a fist into her stomach. She doubled over in pain. He rolled her to her stomach like a rag doll while she was struggling to breathe.

She felt a yank and her wrists being bound behind her back. Her skin burned as the rope tightened.

"You'll never get away with this, Hayden Covey. Attacking me is like hammering another nail in your own coffin. You'll never escape jail now."

"That's not exactly true. They can't tie me to this. I have an alibi. I'm with my football friends. They'll back me, same as always. Besides, you have a madman after you. It will just look like he found you."

"Roy Sales is dead."

"Shut up, you lying bitch."

"I'm not lying. He was killed a few hours ago by the sheriff."

"I don't believe you. I did my homework. I'm setting you on fire, just the way he would have. You could say I'm just helping him out."

Rachel rolled and twisted, fighting to break free as he tied the rough-hewn rope around her ankles. After that he tied the rope to the leg of the heavy wooden table with her fighting him all the way.

He flipped her over, forcing her to watch as he slowly and methodically took a jar from his briefcase.

He opened it and poured a ring of gasoline around her. "Are you ready for some fun, lawyer babe?"

Fear engulfed her. He hadn't even lit a match, but she could already smell the smoke and feel the flames.

She was in hell all over again, but this time Roy Sales was not the ruling demon.

LUKE WAS FIVE miles down the road but still bothered by the fact that his gate had been left open. Cowboys always closed the gate behind them. It was drilled into their minds from the time they were big enough to hop out of the truck and open the gate.

His hired hands had all arrived after the security team left. Who else was on his ranch and why?

He called Rachel. No answer.

Roy Sales was dead. There was no reason to expect that someone else would cause trouble. It likely had something to do with Roy Sales and the evil embedded in him, but Luke couldn't just blow off the open gate.

He had this unwavering hunch that something might be wrong.

He made a U-turn on the narrow road and headed back toward the ranch.

He tried calling Rachel again.

Still no answer. He put the pedal to the metal and practically flew the rest of the way home.

The house looked just as he'd left it. He jumped from his truck and raced up the steps. The front door was ajar even though the temperature was still in the low forties this morning.

The front of the house was empty. He walked back to the kitchen and into hell.

Hayden Covey was standing over Rachel, taunting her with a large, unlit fireplace match, so absorbed in what he was doing that he apparently hadn't heard Luke come in.

Luke pulled his pistol. "Drop that match or I will splatter your brains all over the wall."

Hayden turned toward Luke and went white. The hand that was holding the match began to shake.

Luke expected Hayden to beg for his life. Instead he lit the match. His whole body began to tremble. He was running scared, but he held Rachel's life in his hands.

Luke had been on more dangerous missions in the marines than he could bear to remember. He'd never been truly afraid, never been this scared in all his life.

If Hayden pulled the trigger, the match would still fall into the gasoline. Luke would have seconds to save her from the burst of flames.

He could do it. He'd have to do it.

He cocked his gun.

Hayden heard it and turned. He jumped up and

made a run for the back door, tossing the lit match behind him.

Luke dived into the gasoline in a split second, extinguishing the match before it ignited the fuel and set them all on fire.

Hayden slipped in the liquid. He fell forward, his head bouncing off the edge of the table, knocking him out cold.

Wary, Luke held the gun on him with one hand and pulled a knife from his pocket with the other. He cut the ropes from Rachel's wrists and ankles and the one that bound her to the kitchen table.

"Are you hurt?" Luke asked.

"No. I don't think so unless my heart beats itself out of my chest."

Luke wrapped an arm around her and pulled her close, the gun in his right hand still pointed at Hayden.

Luke tried to speak. There were so many things he wanted to say, but he couldn't get them out. So he did the next best thing. He held Rachel like he'd never let her go.

She lifted her head from Luke's shoulder. "Is Hayden dead?"

"Nope," Luke said. "He's breathing, but he hadn't intended for you to be."

"He definitely meant to kill me. He confessed to murdering Louann before he spread the gasoline."

"Thank God. He left the gate open."

"What?"

"I'll fill you in later," he said. "I think we should call the sheriff now. Our patient is starting to squirm."

"I'll make the call," she said.

Reluctantly, Luke finally let her go. He'd almost lost her. He couldn't imagine a horror worse than that.

The sheriff and two deputies were there in under fifteen minutes. One of the deputies left in an ambulance with Hayden.

By the time the sheriff and his other deputy had done their bit and left, Luke had finally decided what he had to do before he lost his courage.

His dad had never found the right words and he'd admittedly regretted that all his life. Luke wasn't taking that chance, but he didn't know what he'd do if Rachel's answer was no.

He opened his arms and Rachel stepped inside them. "I love you, Rachel. It's probably not the right time or place, but I gotta ask or go crazy. Would you ever consider marrying a cowboy?"

"Absolutely not. Unless that cowboy is you."

"You almost gave me a heart attack."

"The answer is yes. I'll marry you, Luke Dawkins. I love you with all my heart. I don't know how it happened so fast. I only know that it did."

He kissed her, and the promise of forever didn't frighten her at all.

She'd best go shopping for some Western boots. She was home to stay.

* * * * *

SPECIAL EXCERPT FROM

HQN™

Tucker Cahill returns to Gilt Edge, Montana, with no choice but to face down his haunted past when a woman's skeletal remains are found near his family's ranch—but he couldn't have prepared for a young woman seeking vengeance and finding much more.

Read on for a sneak preview of
HERO'S RETURN,
A CAHILL RANCH NOVEL
from New York Times *bestselling author*
B.J. Daniels!

Skeletal Remains Found in Creek

The skeletal remains of a woman believed to be in her late teens or early twenties were discovered in Miner's Creek outside of Gilt Edge, Montana, yesterday. Local coroner Sonny Bates estimated that the remains had been in the creek for somewhere around twenty years.

Sheriff Flint Cahill is looking into missing-persons cases from that time in the hopes of identifying the victim. If anyone has any information, they are encouraged to call the Gilt Edge Sheriff's Department.

"No, Mrs. Kern, I can assure you that the bones that were found in the creek are not those of your nephew Billy," Sheriff Flint Cahill said into the phone at his desk. "I saw Billy last week at the casino. He was alive and well... No, it takes longer than a week for a body to decompose to nothing but bones. Also, the skeletal remains that were found were a young woman's… Yes, Coroner Sonny Bates can tell the difference."

He looked up as the door opened and his sister, Lillie, stepped into his office. From the scowl on her face, he didn't have to ask what kind of mood she was in. He'd been expecting her, given that he had their father locked up in one of the cells.

"Mrs. Kern, I have to go. I'm sorry Billy hasn't called you, but I'm sure he's fine." He hung up with a sigh. "Dad's in the back sleeping it off. Before he passed out, he mumbled about getting back to the mountains."

A very pregnant Lillie nodded but said nothing. Pregnancy had made his sister even prettier. Her long dark hair framed a face that could only be called adorable. This morning, though, he saw something in her gray eyes that worried him.

He waited for her to tie into him, knowing how she felt about him arresting their father for being drunk and disorderly. This wasn't their first rodeo. And like always, it was Lillie who came to bail Ely out—not his bachelor brothers Hawk and Cyrus, who wanted to avoid one of Flint's lectures.

He'd been telling his siblings that they needed to do something about their father. But no one wanted to face the day when their aging dad couldn't continue to spend most of his life in the mountains gold panning and trapping—let alone get a snoot full of booze every time he finally hit town again.

"I'll go get him," Flint said, lumbering to his feet. Since he'd gotten the call about the bones being found at the creek, he hadn't had but a few hours' sleep. All morning, the phone had been ringing off the hook. Not with leads on the identity of the skeletal remains—just residents either being nosy or worried there was a killer on the loose.

"Before you get Dad…" Lillie seemed to hesitate, which wasn't like her. She normally spoke her mind without any encouragement at all.

He braced himself.

"A package came for Tuck."

That was the last thing Flint had expected out of her mouth. "To the saloon?"

"To the ranch. No return address."

Flint felt his heart begin to pound harder. It was the first news of their older brother Tucker since he'd left home right after high school. Being the second oldest, Flint had been closer to Tucker than with his younger brothers. For years, he'd feared him dead. When Tuck had left like that, Flint had suspected his brother was in some kind of trouble. He'd been sure of it. But had it been something bad enough that Tucker hadn't felt he could come to Flint for help?

"Did you open the package?" he asked.

Lillie shook her head. "Hawk and Cyrus thought about it but then called me."

He tried to hide his irritation that one of them had called their sister instead of him, the darned sheriff. His brothers had taken over the family ranch and were the only ones still living on the property, so it wasn't a surprise that they would have received the package. Which meant that whoever had sent it either didn't know that Tucker no longer lived there or they thought he was coming back for some reason.

Because Tucker was on his way home? Maybe he'd sent the package and there was nothing to worry about.

Unfortunately, a package after all this time didn't necessarily bode well. At least not to Flint, who came by his suspicious nature naturally as a lawman. He feared it might be Tucker's last effects.

"I hope *you* didn't open it."

Lillie shook her head. "You think this means he's coming home?" She sounded so hopeful it made his heart ache. He and Tucker had been close in more ways than age. Or at least he'd thought so. But something had been going on with his brother his senior year in high school and Flint had no idea what it was. Or if trouble was still dogging his brother.

For months after Tucker left, Flint had waited for him to return. He'd been so sure that whatever the trouble was, it was temporary. But after all these years, he'd given up any hope. He'd feared he would never see his brother again.

"Tell them not to open it. I'll stop by the ranch and check it out."

Lillie met his gaze. "It's out in my SUV. I brought it with me."

Flint swore under his breath. What if it had a bomb in it? He knew that was overly dramatic, but still, knowing his sister… There wasn't a birthday or Christmas present that she hadn't shaken the life out of as she'd tried to figure out what was inside it. "Is your truck open?" She nodded. "Wait here."

He stepped out into the bright spring day. Gilt Edge sat in a saddle surrounded by four mountain ranges still tipped with snow. Picturesque, tourists came here to fish its blue-ribbon trout stream. But winters were long and a town of any size was a long way off.

Sitting in the middle of Montana, Gilt Edge also had something that most tourists didn't see. It was surrounded by underground missile silos. The one on the Cahill Ranch was renown because that was where their father swore he'd seen a UFO not only land, but also that he'd been forced on board back in 1967. Which had made their father the local crackpot.

Flint took a deep breath, telling himself to relax. His life was going well. He was married to the love of his life. But still, he felt a foreboding that he couldn't shake off. A package for Tucker after all these years?

The air this early in the morning was still cold, but there was a scent to it that promised spring wasn't that far off. He loved spring and summers here and had been looking forward to picnics, trail rides and finishing the yard around the house he and Maggie were building.

He realized that he'd been on edge since he'd gotten the call about the human bones found in the creek. Now he could admit it. He'd felt as if he was waiting for the other shoe to drop. And now this, he thought as he stepped to his sister's SUV.

The box sitting in the passenger-side seat looked battered. He opened the door and hesitated for a moment before picking it up. For its size, a foot-and-half-sized cube, the package was surprisingly light. As he lifted the box out, something shifted inside. The sound wasn't a rattle. It was more a rustle like dead leaves followed by a slight thump.

Like his sister had said, there was no return address. Tucker's name and the ranch address had been neatly printed in black—not in his brother's handwriting. The generic cardboard box was battered enough to suggest it had come from a great distance, but that wasn't necessarily true. It could have looked like that when the sender found it discarded and decided to use it to send the contents. He hesitated for a moment, feeling foolish. But he heard nothing ticking inside. Closing the SUV door, he carried the box inside and put it behind his desk.

"Aren't you going to open it?" Lilly asked, wide-eyed.

"No. You need to take Dad home." He started past his sister but vacillated. "I wouldn't say anything to him about this. We don't want to get his hopes up that Tucker might be headed home. Or make him worry."

She glanced at the box and nodded. "Did you ever understand why Tuck left?"

Flint shook his head. He was torn between anger and sadness when it came to his brother. Also fear. What had happened Tucker's senior year in high school? What if the answer was in that box?

"By the way," he said to his sister, "I didn't arrest Dad. Ely voluntarily turned himself in last night." He shrugged. Flint had never understood his father any more than he had his brother Tuck. To this day, Ely swore that he had been out by the missile silo buried in the middle of their ranch when a UFO landed, took him aboard and did experiments on him.

Then again, their father liked his whiskey and always had.

"You all right?" he asked his sister when she still said nothing.

Lillie nodded distractedly and placed both hands over the baby growing inside her. She was due any day now. He hoped the package for Tucker wasn't something that would hurt his family. He didn't want anything upsetting his sister in her condition. But he could see that just the arrival of the mysterious box had Lillie worried. She wasn't the only one.

TUCKER CAHILL SLOWED his pickup as he drove through Gilt Edge. He'd known it would be emotional, returning after all these years. He'd never doubted he would return—he just hadn't expected it to take nineteen years. All that time, he'd been waiting like a man on death row, knowing how it would eventually end.

Still, he was filled with a crush of emotion. *Home.* He hadn't realized how much he'd missed it, how much he'd missed his family, how much he'd missed his life in Montana. He'd been waiting for this day, dreading it and, at the same time, anxious to return at least once more.

As he started to pull into a parking place in front of the sheriff's department, he saw a pregnant woman come out followed by an old man with long gray hair and a beard. His breath caught. Not sure if he was more shocked to see how his father had aged—or how pregnant and grown up his little sister, Lillie, was now.

He couldn't believe it as he watched Lillie awkwardly climb into an SUV, the old man going around to the passenger side. He felt his heart swell at the sight of them. Lillie had been nine when he'd left. But he could never forget a face that adorable. Was that really his father? He couldn't believe it. When had Ely Cahill become an old mountain man?

He wanted to call out to them but stopped himself. As much as he couldn't wait to see them, there was something he had to take care of first. Tears burned his eyes as he watched Lillie drive their father away. It appeared he was about to be an uncle. Over the years while he was hiding out, he'd made a point of following what news he could from Gilt Edge. He'd missed so much with his family.

He swallowed the lump in his throat as he opened his pickup door and stepped out. The good news was that his brother Flint was sheriff. That, he hoped, would make it easier to do what he had to do. But facing Flint after all this time away... He knew he owed his family an explanation, but Flint more than the rest. He and his brother had been so close—until his senior year.

He braced himself as he pulled open the door to the sheriff's department and stepped in. He'd let everyone down nineteen years ago, Flint especially. He doubted his brother would have forgotten—or forgiven him.

But that was the least of it, Flint would soon learn.

AFTER HIS SISTER LEFT, Flint moved the battered cardboard box to the corner of his desk. He'd just pulled out his pocketknife to cut through the tape when his intercom buzzed.

"There's a man here to see you," the dispatcher said. He could hear the hesitation in her voice. "He says he's your *brother*?" His family members never had the dispatcher announce them. They just came on back to his office. *"Your brother, Tucker?"*

Flint froze for a moment. Hands shaking, he laid down his pocketknife as relief surged through him. Tucker was alive and back in Gilt Edge? He had to clear his throat before he said, "Send him in."

He told himself he wasn't prepared for this and yet it was something he'd dreamed of all these years. He stepped around to the front of his desk, half-afraid of what to expect. A lot could have happened to his brother in nineteen years. The big question, though, was why come back now?

As a broad-shouldered cowboy filled his office doorway, Flint blinked. He'd been expecting the worst.

Instead, Tucker looked great. Still undeniably handsome with his thick dark hair and gray eyes like the rest of the Cahills, Tucker had filled out from the teenager who'd left home. Wherever he'd been, he'd apparently fared well. He appeared to have been doing a lot of physical labor, because he was buff and tanned.

Flint was overwhelmed by both love and regret as

he looked at Tuck, and furious with him for making him worry all these years.

"Hello, Flint," Tucker said, his voice deeper than Flint remembered.

He couldn't speak for a moment, afraid of what would come out of his mouth. The last thing he wanted to do was drive his brother away again. He wanted to hug him and slug him at the same time.

Instead, he said, voice breaking, "Tuck. It's so damned good to see you," and closed the distance between them to pull his older brother into a bear hug.

TUCKER HUGGED FLINT, fighting tears. It had been so long. Too long. His heart broke at the thought of the lost years. But Flint looked good, taller than Tucker remembered, broader shouldered, too.

"When did you get so handsome?" Tucker said as he pulled back, his eyes still burning with tears. It surprised him that they were both about the same height. Like him, Flint had filled out. With their dark hair and gray eyes, they could almost pass for twins.

The sheriff laughed. "You know darned well that you're the prettiest of the bunch of us."

Tucker laughed, too, at the old joke. It felt good. Just like it felt good to be with family again. "Looks like you've done all right for yourself."

Flint sobered. "I thought I'd never see you again."

"Like Dad used to say, I'm like a bad penny. I'm

bound to turn up. How is the old man? Was that him I saw leaving with Lillie?"

"You didn't talk to them?" Flint sounded both surprised and concerned.

"I wanted to see you first." Tucker smiled as Flint laid a hand on his shoulder and squeezed gently before letting go.

"You know how he was after Mom died. Now he spends almost all of his time up in the mountains panning gold and trapping. He had a heart attack a while back, but it hasn't slowed him down. There's no talking any sense into him."

"Never was." Tucker nodded as a silence fell between them. He and Flint had once been so close. Regret filled him as Flint studied him for a long moment before he stepped back and motioned him toward a chair in his office.

Closing the door, Flint settled into his chair behind his desk. Tucker dragged up one of the office chairs.

"I wondered if you wouldn't be turning up, since Lillie brought in a package addressed to you when she came to pick up Dad. He often spends a night in my jail when he's in town. Drunk and disorderly."

Tucker didn't react to that. He was looking at the battered brown box sitting on Flint's desk. *"A package?"* His voice broke. No one could have known he was coming back here unless...

Don't miss
HERO'S RETURN,
available March 2018 wherever
HQN Books and ebooks are sold.

www.Harlequin.com

Get 2 Free Books,
Plus 2 Free Gifts—
just for trying the Reader Service!

"I had nowhere else to go." Her words came out in a rush. "I was so
worried that you wouldn't be here." She burst into tears and slumped
as if physically exhausted.

He caught her, swung her up into his arms and carried her into the
house, kicking the door closed behind him. His mind raced as he tried
to imagine what could have happened to bring her to his door in Gilt
Edge, Montana, in the middle of the night and in this condition.

"Sit here," he said as he carried her in and set her down in a kitchen
chair before going for the first-aid kit. When he returned, he was
momentarily taken aback by the memory of this woman the first time
he'd met her. She wasn't beautiful in the classic sense. But she was
striking, from her wide violet eyes fringed with pale lashes to the silk
of her long blond hair. She had looked like an angel, especially in the
long white dress she'd been wearing that night.

That was over a year ago and he hadn't seen her since. Nor had he
expected to since they'd met initially several hundred miles from the
ranch. But whatever had struck him about her hadn't faded. There was
something flawless about her—even as scraped up and bruised as she
was. It made him furious at whoever was responsible for this.

"Can you tell me what happened?" he asked as he began to clean
the cuts.

"I…I…" Her throat seemed to close on a sob.

HIEXP0418

"It's okay, don't try to talk." He felt her trembling and could see that she was fighting tears. "This cut under your eye is deep."

She said nothing, looking as if it was all she could do to keep her eyes open. He took in her torn and filthy dress. It was long, like the white one he'd first seen her in, but faded. It reminded him of something his grandmother might have worn to do housework in. She was also thinner than he remembered.

As he gently cleaned her wounds, he could see dark circles under her eyes, and her long braided hair was in disarray with bits of twigs and leaves stuck in it.

The night he'd met her, her plaited hair had been pinned up at the nape of her neck—until he'd released it, the blond silk dropping to the center of her back.

He finished his doctoring, put away the first-aid kit and wondered how far she'd come to find him and what she had been through to get here. When he returned to the kitchen, he found her standing at the back window, staring out. As she turned, he saw the fear in her eyes—and the exhaustion.

Colt desperately wanted to know what had happened to her and how she'd ended up on his doorstep. He hadn't even thought that she'd known his name. "Have you had anything to eat?"

"Not in the past forty-eight hours or so," she said, squinting at the clock on the wall as if not sure what day it was. "And not all that much before that."

He'd been meaning to get into Gilt Edge and buy some groceries. "Sit and I'll see what I can scare up," he said as he opened the refrigerator. Seeing only one egg left, he said, "How do you feel about pancakes? I have chokecherry syrup."

She nodded and attempted a smile. She looked skittish as a newborn calf. Worse, he sensed that she was having second thoughts about coming here.

She licked her cracked lips. "I have to tell you. I have to explain—"

"It's okay. You're safe here."

Don't miss
COWBOY'S REDEMPTION by B.J. Daniels,
available May 2018 wherever
Harlequin Intrigue® books and ebooks are sold.

www.Harlequin.com

HIEXP0418

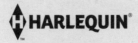